I0688292

James Payn

The burnt million by James Payn

Vol. II

James Payn

The burnt million by James Payn
Vol. II

ISBN/EAN: 9783743377196

Manufactured in Europe, USA, Canada, Australia, Japa

Cover: Foto ©Andreas Hilbeck / pixelio.de

Manufactured and distributed by brebook publishing software (www.brebook.com)

James Payn

The burnt million by James Payn

THE BURNT MILLION

BY

JAMES PAYN

AUTHOR OF 'BY PROXY' ETC.

IN THREE VOLUMES

VOL. II.

London

CHATTO & WINDUS, PICCADILLY

1890

PRINTED BY
SPOTTISWOODE AND CO., NEW-STREET SQUARE
LONDON

CONTENTS

OF

THE SECOND VOLUME

THE BURNT MILLION

CHAPTER XVIII

CONFIDENCES

ALTHOUGH Lord Cheribert was not a boating-man, he was well acquainted with river life; he had a natural tendency towards sport of every description; and, to say the truth, cared for little else. It is often said of this and that clever young fellow who shoots, or rides, or even plays whist or billiards to admiration, that the talents he exhibits in these pursuits would, properly directed, lead him to fame or fortune; but the fact is, some men are born with a marvellous capacity for sports

and games, and for nothing else. That pupil
of Plato's whom the philosopher would have

> Formed for virtue's nobler view
> By precept and example too,

but who *would* persist in astonishing the
crowd at the Corinthian games by his skill
as a whip (which must have been considerable), was one of this class. Though he
could make the wheels of his four-in-hand

> Along the indented plain, the self-same track to mark again,

it is probable he could never have pursued
even a single course of philosophic lectures.
The thing was not in him; he was born for a
life of pleasure. A contemptible existence, it
may be said, enough; but, on the other hand,
it is to be noted that your born sportsman (in
the English, not the American sense) is not
always an idle man, and does not necessarily
turn out the total wreck and failure that a
man of pleasure who is not a sportsman is
almost sure to become. He may be dissipated,

but he need not be debauched ; he may be reckless, but he is rarely callous ; he may easily enough, under adverse circumstances, be a scamp, but there is generally something wholesome about him which preserves him from being a scoundrel.

Lord Cheribert was a man of this kind ; but though he had no aptitude for the serious business of life, he had gifts which would have made him a social success—would have ensured him, that is, a personal popularity in any branch of it. Being a lord and the heir to a great estate, his gracious manners and handsome face, his humour and frankness, would have made him a *persona grata* with society could he have been induced to mingle with it; but society bored him. Compared with the ordinary devotees of the turf, who had been his chosen companions, he seemed like an angel, though undoubtedly a fallen one ; with them he was like the one-eyed man among the blind. But to those who knew nothing about

his antecedents—and even to some who did—
he was, superficially, very attractive. He had
the art of making himself agreeable without
exertion in a high degree. With women he
was an immense favourite ; and he was no
more capable of behaving dishonourably to
them than he was of theft.

Though, as we have said, not aquatic, he
was conversant with boating matters, and in
one half-hour put his audience so much *au
courant* with everything in connection with
them, that the changing scenes of river life
constantly presented to their eyes were
invested with thrice the attraction they had
hitherto possessed for them.

'I know Elm Place quite well,' he said ;
' Villiers had it, you know' (here he turned to
Mr. Roscoe), 'who came to grief over Camper-
down at Doncaster.'

Mr. Roscoe nodded ; he could have given
other causes for Mr. Villiers having come to
grief, had he so chosen.

'Indeed,' continued the young fellow, 'I have lunched before' (for they were now partaking of that meal) 'in this very room,' and he looked round him with an air of reminiscence.

It was a large apartment, with four French windows, all now open, so that, except for the comfort with which the meal was served, it might have been a picnic. 'To my mind it is the pleasantest house upon the river, though that roar of the Milton Weir has always a melancholy sound to my ears.'

'I rather like it,' said Agnes; 'it reminds me of the London traffic, which, when one is away from town, one somehow always misses.'

'And you, Miss Grace?' inquired Lord Cheribert.

'Yes, I like it too. There is something soothing, if a little sullen, in that eternity of sound.'

'I used to like it once myself,' said the

young man gravely; 'but for me it has now a tragic association.'

'Really? Oh, do tell us!' exclaimed Philippa. 'I do so love tragedy.'

This was not true, for incidents of a tragic nature 'upset' her. It will be remembered how dreadfully 'cut up,' as Mr. Roscoe had expressed it, she had been on the occasion of her father's death, though she had since come to regard her loss with a little too much philosophy. She was more emotional than Agnes, and certainly more easily frightened. When she said she loved a tragedy, she only meant that she was curious to know what had happened at the weir. The river forked at Milton Weir, where a few posts marked out the course of its main current; the side stream rushed through these posts at speed, and then with increased velocity dashed over the weir in foam and thunder.

'Well, it is rather a sad story to tell people at lunch,' said Lord Cheribert unwillingly; 'but I suppose such things are constantly happening on the river; there is scarcely an eddy which has not had its victim or a bathing-place where somebody has not been drowned; only I saw this with my own eyes, you see, which makes a difference. We were sitting at this very table—a whole lot of us—when an argument arose about boating. Some said you could "shoot" Milton Weir, and others that you could not, and then the speed and force of the by-stream, that leads to the lock, were discussed, and whether a good swimmer could hold his own in it. Young Picton, of the Guards, said he was sure it could be done, and offered to back himself to pass the posts, and swim round the one which stands with a ring through it, about thirty yards further down, in the very centre of the stream, and back again. It seemed rather a foolhardy thing to try, but he said he had been in worse places in the river (though it would be difficult to find them), and I took odds that he would do it. I regret that bet to this day.'

'Still, as you were backing him,' observed Mr. Roscoe, 'it could not have influenced him in any way to undertake the matter.'

'I am not sure,' said the young lord gloomily; 'if there had been no backers there would have been no layers, and I put a pony on it. A lot of us went off to the place at once in a couple of punts; young Picton was in my boat, in the highest spirits. He was not twenty, and as fine a young fellow as there was in the regiment. When he had stripped, and just before he took his header, he called out: "Get your money ready, I shall be back under the ten minutes." But he never came back to us alive.'

'How horrible!' exclaimed Grace with a shudder.

'Why, yes, as it turned out,' assented Lord Cheribert in a gentle and contrite tone; 'but nothing was further from our thoughts than his being drowned. He might not get round the middle post, which he had backed himself to do, but we thought he would at least be drawn down by the current to the weir, where there is a landing-stage. But that by-stream is full of under-currents, as we were afterwards told, and the poor boy, though he got round the post, was whirled round and round before our eyes, and presently pulled under as though a rope had been tied to his legs. When the place was dragged for him, it was found choked with water-weeds, and he among them. And that is why I don't like the sound of the Milton Weir.'

The ladies looked greatly horrified, and there was an unpleasant silence at the conclusion of the young lord's narrative. Mr. Roscoe broke it by observing dryly, 'But you won your bet?'

'I won it, but I did not take it,' replied Lord Cheribert. 'As the other man was obliged, of course, to pay, I sent the hundred pounds—for he had bet me 4 to 1—to the Royal Humane Society. I was more sentimental at that time than since you have known me, Mr. Roscoe,' he added sharply.

'It was quite the right thing to do,' said that gentleman with undisturbed serenity.

'If you think so, that, of course, settles the question.'

The young man was rather ashamed of the weakness he had exhibited, and resented exceedingly the other's cynical comment. His irritation was so far of advantage, that the spectacle of it turned the thoughts of the ladies from the tragic episode he had been describing, and Agnes, with some tact, began to praise the Royal Humane Society, and then, gradually extricating herself from the subject, proposed a walk in the grounds.

She was a clever woman, though her sympathies were restricted within narrow limits. Her natural horror at the incident just described had already quitted her, as water slips from a duck's back; though it was not so with Philippa, and much less with Grace, whose face still wore an expression of distress and pain. Lord Cheribert was angry with himself, as Agnes saw, for having evoked it.

'Do you know the view from the hill at the back of the house?' she asked him. 'Grace has made some sketches of it; show them to Lord Cheribert, my dear.'

The sketches were sent for and duly admired.

'They are charming,' said the young man; 'would it be rude to ask if they are truthful?'

'You are putting the artist on the horns of a dilemma,' put in Agnes, smiling; 'she must either confess to failure or run the risk of being thought conceited.'

'You are quite right,' said the young man humbly. 'I am always making a fool of myself. Let us go up the hill by all means.'

Then it so happened that Agnes and Philippa had some alteration to make in their toilettes, while Grace had none; so Lord Cheribert and herself started a little in advance of them, Mr. Roscoe, of course, delaying for the two elder ladies, on one or other of whom he was in constant attendance.

'I hope I have not shocked you too much with my sad tale, Miss Grace,' said the young lord, in a tone of tender apology, as they walked up the hill.

'I was shocked, I confess, Lord Cheribert.'

'I do not wonder at it; I was wrong to tell the story. It is a terrible thing for a fine young fellow to be cut off like that.'

'For a bet,' observed Grace with severity.

'Yes, and, as you say, for a bet. I used to bet a good deal, as I dare say you have heard.'

'I have heard something about it.'

'Well, I don't do it now; at least I don't mean to do it after next month.'

'Why next month?'

'Because that is when my race comes off, you know; or rather you don't know. It is very much after time. I have promised my father that it shall be my last professional performance on the pig—I mean in the saddle.'

'Do you mean that you are a professional jockey?'

'Well, no; not quite that,' he answered, smiling; 'there are gentlemen riders of course. You seem to be quite ignorant of those things; most of the ladies I know—but, to be sure, I don't know many—are devoted to racing.'

'And to bets?'

'Yes, and to bets. Of course some of them only bet gloves—these always want a point or two, I notice, beyond the odds; but some of them make regular books, and are quite as keen about the money as we are.'

'I don't think I should like those ladies.'

'I dare say not; I am not wildly fond of

them myself. I prefer quiet girls, who have good feelings and—and—what a dear doggie that is of yours! Rip, Rip!' and the little creature barked and danced around the young lord, just as he would have had him to do, and so preserved him from a very considerable embarrassment. Grace had by no means fallen in love with him, as perhaps he flattered himself, and was not embarrassed in the least. If she had understood his meaning, as he now felt, she might not only have been embarrassed but even angry; he had been going much too quick and too far, but Rip had saved him. Dogs have great sagacity; in Hampshire they are trained for truffle-hunting: why should they not be also trained for 'gooseberry picking'—to accompany young people in the early days of their 'walking' together, and to make diversions just at the right moment?

'Since you disapprove of those who are keen, as you express it, about winning money from their friends, Lord Cheribert,' said Grace after a pause, 'why do you like to do it yourself?'

'I was only speaking of the matter as regards ladies, Miss Grace. With a man, of course, it is different. What is a fellow to do—I mean a fellow in my position—if he does not speculate a little? I don't understand investments, as your poor father did, so I try the turf, not with such satisfactory results, I am sorry to say.' He was defending himself by this reference to Mr. Tremenhere, but he little knew the effectiveness of his weapon. She took a milder view of the young man's proceedings at once, though he had not her father's excellent motives.

'Yes, I suppose the desire of gain is natural to a man,' she said, 'like his delight in hunting. I can't understand the attraction in either case, so I suppose I am no judge of it. You don't want the money and you don't want the fox.'

'Oh, but there you are quite mistaken, Miss Grace,' he put in earnestly. 'As to the fox, I have not a word to say; he has a disagreeable smell, which the money never has—even the old Romans knew that—*non olet*, they said—and I want it exceedingly. Considering what people are pleased to call my " position," I am the greatest pauper in all England.'

'You don't look like it,' answered Grace, smiling. His frankness and the smile that so well suited it were having their effect upon her.

'Well, these flannels are not costly, though my tailor will have to wait for his money for them. But it is the very fact of one's having to keep up a certain appearance that prevents one from retrenching: at least that is what the governor says in explanation of what Mr. Roscoe would call a tightness in the money market. I am ashamed of myself for speaking of such matters to you, Miss Grace; but if any one should ever tell you that I am exceedingly hard up, I am sorry to say—whatever might be their motive for saying it—that they would only be saying the truth.'

She looked at him in some surprise, for his tone seemed unnecessarily earnest.

'I don't suppose anyone is likely to say anything of the kind to me, Lord Cheribert.'

'Very likely not,' he laughed uneasily; 'but if they do, you know, you might just tell them that you had been made aware of the fact by the person principally interested. Now I dare say you are saying to yourself what an egotistic creature this man is to bore me with his private affairs, in which I cannot see one ray of interest.'

'Nay, Lord Cheribert, that is not so,' she answered gently; 'but, no doubt through my own stupidity, I am utterly unable to understand the immense importance which people, who have enough to live upon, attach to more money.'

'Indeed!' He looked surprised in his turn. 'Well, the fact is, I am not in a position to enlighten you upon that point,' replied the young fellow, laughing, 'for I have never *had* enough to live upon. I have been in debt ever since I was at school.'

'That means that you have always lived beyond your income, and, I am afraid, been very extravagant,' she answered reprovingly.

'People do say that,' he admitted gravely, 'but then they will say anything. Selwyn says—but perhaps you don't know Selwyn—that if you spend every shilling on yourself it is quite extraordinary how far your money can be made to go; but I protest I never found it so.'

'And have you spent every shilling on yourself, Lord Cheribert?'

'Directly or indirectly, every sixpence.'

'Then you must forgive me for saying that I think it shameful. Some of us err in that way through ignorance of what is going on in the world, but that cannot be your case. Pray Heaven for a human heart, my lord.'

As she stood regarding him, face to face, with a flush of indignation on her cheek, and the fire of scorn in her eyes, he stared at her in amazement.

'My heart is human enough, Miss Grace,' he answered humbly, 'and I don't think it is hard.'

'Pardon me; I had no right to speak so, Lord Cheribert.'

'Nay pardon *me*; you have a right, if you will permit me to say that much. But I don't think I am quite so worthless as I seem.' She would have spoken, but he stopped her with a gesture. 'Pray listen to me one moment in my own defence. There are those who will tell you that I have had great advantages, and therefore ought to be a better man. I ought, Heaven knows, but not on that account. I have had *dis*advantages of every kind. Spoilt from my cradle, fawned upon even in boyhood, which it is most falsely told us is the age of naturalness, flattered as I grew up, to the top of my bent, I have never heard the truth about myself, till now, from a single voice, save one, and that a harsh one —my own father's.'

'Had you no mother?' inquired Grace softly.

'She died before I knew her.'

'So did mine,' murmured the girl.

'But you, at least, had a father who loved you dearly. That was not my case. I do not know when it was that he began to look coldly upon me, but it was too early. I was one to be led, I think—I could never stand being driven—but there was no one to lead me; and now, perhaps, it is too late.'

Grace trembled, but not, as the young man perhaps imagined, from any notion of taking him in hand; she trembled at her audacity in having taken it upon herself to lecture him. She felt like a timid school-mistress who has 'tackled' too big a boy.

'I understand,' she said, 'you have been reconciled to your father.'

'Yes, that is so, in a sort of way. He means to be kind now, I think—after next month.'

'Next month ?'

'Yes, after my last race is ridden. His paternal heart will not begin to yearn for me till I have left the turf. Mr. Allerton will tell you all about it, if you are so good as to ask him.'

The young girl blushed on her own account for the first time. She recognised at once that there could be only one reason for her making inquiry of Mr. Allerton about Lord Cheribert's prospects of amendment, and, above all, for his asking her to do so. The young man perceived her embarrassment and at once endeavoured to relieve it.

'Perhaps some day or other, Miss Grace,'

he continued, smiling, 'I shall be a pattern son and a reformed character, and you will say "Good boy" instead of scolding me.'

'I never meant to scold you; I had no right——'

'You said that before,' he put in quickly; 'I hope you will not repeat it. It is the only thing you have said to me that was not kind.—Rip! Rip! good doggie! so they are coming up, are they?—How quick his ears are for the feet of a friend! Here are your sisters and Mr. Roscoe.'

CHAPTER XIX

THE WEIR

OF all pleasure-vessels, there is none so much run down—though it has the reputation of doing that to others—as the river steam-launch. It is too big for its place; it is ugly; its voice is strident and ear-piercing; and it causes waves to rise in its wake that are a great nuisance to rowing-boats. All this is very true; but, for comfort and convenience to its passengers, give me (or even lend me) a steam-launch, in preference to any other boat that cleaves the stream. There are no per-spiring rowers to watch, which of itself is a relief to anyone gifted with human pity; you can move about without upsetting the ship, or shipping a sea, or unshipping the rudder, or doing anything nautically objectionable; you have not got to look out (metaphorically speaking) for squalls; another has to look out for *you*—and squalls; you can take your lunch like a civilised being, and a much better one than ever came out of a rowboat; you are not concerned about the difference between up-stream and down-stream; you 'need no aid of sail or oar, and heed no spite of wind or tide'; and when it rains you can get under cover.

Of course there was a steam-launch attached to Elm Place, as well as a flotilla of skiffs and punts; its name was the *Comet*, but when the Tremenheres used it it was more commonly termed the *Compassion*, because of its gentle ways. Grace would never go on board of it save under a solemn promise that it should not spurt unless the course was clear; that it should 'slow' whenever there was a boat within fifty yards of it; and that it should never be allowed to scream. When it wanted the lock gates open a horn was blown, *vice* the steam-whistle superseded. This made it a floating heaven for everybody as well as the angel herself. Sometimes the *Compassion* would tow a boat or two up-stream, when the joy and gratitude of the tired oarsmen were delightful to see, and proved what they really thought of rowing.

Lord Cheribert, in spite of his flannels, was never unwilling to forego the delights of boating and accept an invitation from the ladies to go up or down the river in the *Comet*. He generally had a bet or two with Mr. Roscoe—just a sovereign or so, unless that gentleman thought it a particularly 'good thing,' when he would 'make it a fiver'— about how many boats there would be in a lock, or how many swans they would meet in a mile—for he could no more help betting than he could help breathing; it was not, however, that time was heavy on his hands, for he enjoyed these little trips amazingly, and had an idea that he was getting domestic. His company was greatly appreciated by Mr. Roscoe, because he won money of him ; by the two elder sisters, because he was a lord (they would have liked to have had painted on him—as the boat had the *Comet* on her stern—' This is a lord ') ; and by Grace, because she really liked him.   His manners were unexceptionable ; his talk was bright and genial ; and she believed that he had a good heart. Perhaps he had ; it ought at all events to be in good condition, for it had suffered nothing from use.   It had experienced a few impulses —some creditable to him, but some the reverse—that was all. Grace likened him with the poet to the lily.

Lord Cheribert, though no profligate, was not, it must be confessed, much like that emblem of purity in other respects.   He once told an old friend of hers with whom he was acquainted, in an unwonted moment of confidence, that Grace Tremenhere ' did him good'; and in a vague sort of way, I think, she shared this notion. There is nothing so pleasing to a girl's nature as the belief that she is reforming a rake, though, as a general rule, she might as well stroke a hedgehog with the object of making that animal smooth. Grace did not flatter herself to this extent; but it did not escape her observation that in her presence the young fellow was always at his best; that he toned himself down, as it were—'slowed' like the *Comet*—and strove to make his conversation agreeable to her. She sighed over him while she smiled at him. Her sisters often interchanged significant glances in connection with these young people, and even whispered to one another:

'I really think this will come to something.'

Mr. Roscoe nodded agreement, and, with less circumlocution, observed, 'He's hooked'—an expression more forcible than appropriate, since it suggested that the young lady had been fishing for him, which was very far indeed from being the case.

A great deal of river life was seen from the deck of the *Comet*, and a very picturesque and pleasant spectacle it was. Grace grew quite learned about it, thanks to Lord Cheribert's teaching, who enjoyed his tutorship amazingly, and could not understand what the poor devils had to complain about who found coaching so irksome; he would have taught her anything he knew with the same alacrity, though the terms of payment were less distinctly understood than he could have wished.

Their neighbours at Milton in the aquatic line particularly interested the ladies; it is a village as completely given up to boating-men in the summer months as Switzerland is to tourists. Every day fifty fine young fellows, in every description of river craft, from the punt to the canoe, set forth from it up stream or down, and many of their sunburnt faces grew quite familiar to them. The two London eight-oars were their favourite boats, the crews of which were probably even more familiar with them, though neither party had interchanged a word. Whether in acknowledgment of the courtesy exercised by the *Compassion* in 'slowing' or from the natural chivalry of their disposition, these young gentlemen would often get up a race for the amusement of its owners, and in return the launch would sometimes tow them home. When this happened the ladies had an opportunity of observing their unknown friends with considerable particularity. At first the *Monarch* used to beat the *Prudent*, but after a while the result of the struggle was the other way, in consequence, as Lord Cheribert said, of a change in the latter's crew. The new stroke was a stranger to him, but he had heard something about him, and indeed it was natural to those who saw Walter Sinclair for the first time to inquire who he was. He was not only a tall powerful young fellow, exceptionally good-looking—fair except as to face and hands, which the sun had tanned to a tawny hue, and with nut-brown hair that seemed to curl more and more as he warmed to his work—but he had an air of great distinction. Though evidently a gentleman, he had not the aristocratic appearance of Lord Cheribert; but his expression, which is unusual among boating men, was curiously thoughtful. When he was pulling he pulled with a will—or, as Mr. Roscoe expressed it, ‘ like ten thousand devils ’—but when in repose he seemed to lose himself. He seldom joined in the subdued talk and laughter of the rest of the crew at their ease; his grey eyes seemed to be looking into space for something beyond the horizon. Yet they took in everything about him—he was the best ‘ look-out ’ in the boat—and sometimes (though he was much too well bred to stare) they took in the *Comet*, every stick of her, like a flash of

lightning. He interested the ladies consider-
ably, who named him Werter from his supposed disposition to melancholy; but whether
he was so or not, he was certainly the cause
of melancholy to the *Monarch*. Lord Cheribert affirmed that he was as good a swimmer
as he was an oarsman, and that he could give
any of his companions ten yards in a hundred
in a foot-race. *They* called him *the Cherokee*,
because he had been amongst the American
Indians, and had acquired some of their
accomplishments.

One afternoon the *Comet* made rather a
longer voyage than usual, down to Windsor;
it was a day Grace long remembered. Never
had the river looked so bright and joyous.
She could scarcely tell whether the warmth
of the sunshine in the open, or the chequered
shadow of the woods, or the coolness of the
locks, as the launch sank with the sinking of
the waters, was most delightful. The Castle,
seen from the bosom of Father Thames—the

noblest spectacle that man's hand has ever given to man's eye—the woods of Cliefden, not yet touched with autumn's fiery finger; the peaceful villages on either side the stream, had never seemed to her so beautiful. Lord Cheribert sat near her quietly smoking the contents of his cigar-case, which was of the size of a small portmanteau; if he could not always sympathise with her thoughts, he knew when she did not want them disturbed, and found satisfaction enough in looking at her as she sat with Rip on her lap, and her dreamy eyes half closed. There are eyes which, though beautiful in themselves, look better so, as Solomon (who had a great ex- perience) well understood: they take us with their lids. Presently the dog leaped down and began to bark; a swan was hissing at someone in a canoe. It was ungrateful of the bird, for the man had been feeding her with biscuits, and when his store was finished, and he moved lightly away with a silvery splash of his oar, she resented it. It was Werter, as they called him, returning home and close to Milton lock. Its gates received his canoe, as well as the launch, into its icy bosom, which slowly rose with both of them. There are few places where we get so good a view of our fellow-creatures as when we are in the same lock with them; it is almost as good as being in the same boat.

'What a magnificent fellow that Sinclair is!' observed Lord Cheribert softly; 'it is a pity that Oxford could not have him in their boat at Putney.'

'He is not a University man, then?' inquired Grace.

'Oh, no; he has had a rough time of it in his life, I believe, out in the Wild West.'

'He does not look rough.'

'No, indeed. He is gentle and good-natured enough, they tell me.'

Here the young fellow put his hand upon the launch to steady his frail craft, and Rip, having sniffed at it as if it were something nice to eat, proceeded to lick his fingers.

'It is a good sign when your little dog takes to a man, Miss Grace, is it not?' whispered Lord Cheribert.

'I don't think Mr. Roscoe would agree with that sentiment,' answered the girl, smiling. 'But nevertheless, generally speaking, I think it is so.'

'I'm glad to hear you say that, because, you know, he took to *me*.' And he looked up in Grace's face and smiled his sunniest smile.

The lock gates opened slowly, making their wooden frame as usual for the river picture, and out came steam-launch and canoe together, side by side. Then a sad mischance happened. It was at Milton lock, it will be remembered, where the by-stream ran down to the river at mill-race speed. The great posts just marked the road for the river craft, and on the other side of them the current seethed and boiled, as if mad to join in the headlong leap of the water.

Just as Sinclair pushed off, the dog, unwilling as it seemed to lose his new friend, overbalanced himself, and fell into the water. Grace saw it and sprang up with a scream of horror, and everyone started up aghast to see what had happened. Poor Rip, though swimming his best against his fate, was violently carried by the stream between the posts; and the next moment there was a great splash in the water and the canoe turned bottom upwards: Sinclair had jumped out of it after the dog. It was a generous impulse, but, to one who knew the river, seemed little short of the act of a madman.

'The weeds! the weeds!' exclaimed Lord Cheribert at the top of his voice. 'There are weeds under the left bank!'

If the swimmer heard he did not heed, for to the left bank the dog was being hurried, and after him he made. It was a most exciting, but, to those who had heard Lord Cheribert's story of that very place, a very distressing spectacle. The young fellow swam like a fish; in half a dozen powerful strokes he had overtaken the little half-drowned creature, and, reversing the usual practice in such cases of emergency, the man had seized the dog's neck with his teeth and held him up above the waves. As with his strange burden the young fellow turned about, with shining face, a shout of applause burst from all beholders. The next moment it died away, and was succeeded by a shudder of fear. Instead of swimming towards the weir, where there was a landing-stage, as all ex-pected, he made for the post and ring that stood in the centre of the by-stream; and after a stroke or two, though he still moved his powerful arms, they perceived that he was not only making no progress, but sinking lower in the water. The weeds, the presence of which had cut him off from the weir, had got him by the leg. It was a terrible moment. Agnes and Philippa hid their faces; Grace, white as death, with parted lips and staring eyes looked on in speechless agony. Lord Cheribert kicked off his shoes.

'No, my lord,' whispered Roscoe, seizing his arm and holding it as in a vice, 'you shall *not*: it would be certain death to you, and he is as good as dead already.'

But Sinclair was not dead. With a last almost superhuman effort he suddenly freed himself from the weeds, and, still with the dog in his mouth, reached the post, and seized the ring. Then the men cheered and the women wept.

'There's not another man in England who could have done it,' exclaimed Lord Cheribert admiringly, 'or who would not have let go of the dog.'

The next moment the young fellow was sitting on the post with the dog in his arms. He took off his cap, which had somehow stuck to him throughout, and tossed it in the air. Every man burst out laughing, not so much at the absurdity of the spectacle as a relief to their feelings: in the laughter of the two elder ladies there was, however, much more of hysterics than mirth, and Grace did not laugh at all. She was greatly distressed and pained, but she took out her pocket-handkerchief, and waved it in reply to the young man's salutation. The thunder of the weir made any verbal communication with him from anybody out of the question.

Then the lock-keeper put out in a punt attached to the bank by a long chain, and delivered the youth from his unpleasant situation, where he was sitting, however, quite at his ease. Rip half drowned, and a quarter frightened to death, was shivering in silence; he had not a bark left in him. The lock-keeper would have taken the dog, but Sinclair kept hold of it, and, walking quietly down to the river-side where the launch awaited him, was about to hand the animal to Lord Cheribert, as though returning some little article which he had picked up, when Grace interfered and held out her trembling hands.

'I am afraid he is rather wet,' said the young fellow, smiling. He was rather wet himself, but looked not a whit the worse for that.

'How very, very good and wrong of you!' she murmured earnestly, as, hugging her little favourite with one hand, she held out the other to him with a tearful smile; she was what Philippa afterwards termed 'very much upset.'

Then Agnes, perceiving her sister's embarrassment, stepped forward and said, 'You have done a very fine, but, I am obliged to add, a very foolish thing, sir; to have saved our dog at the risk of your own life. I really don't know *what* to say to you.' .

'You can ask him to dinner,' observed Lord Cheribert sententiously.

'We shall be delighted to see you if you will come over to " The Place "; we dine at even,' said Agnes graciously.

'I am afraid I have no dinner *dress*,' replied the young fellow ruefully.

'That is not of the least consequence,' observed the hostess.

'You must change *that* at all events,' remarked his lordship, pointing to his dripping garments, ' or I shall dine in a mackintosh. Mr. Roscoe and I will call for you in half an hour.'

CHAPTER XX

WALTER SINCLAIR

SOME people would have called Lord Cheribert's conduct in proposing that Walter Sinclair should be invited to Elm Place little short of chivalrous; when a young man is seeking the affections of a young woman, and has not yet obtained them, he is not generally so willing that she should cultivate an acquaintance with a possible rival. But the fact is that the idea of rivalship never entered into Lord Cheribert's head. It is one of the advantages of being a lord that that position gives one a great sense of security. The young fellow was fully persuaded, though he had not yet succeeded in recommending himself to Grace as a suitor, that there was no one else who was preferred to him ; and it never struck him for a moment that Mr. Walter Sinclair should be preferred. He himself had a liking for the man, admired his good looks, his prominence in all athletic exercises, the pluck he had exhibited—and perhaps still more the recklessness—in saving the life of the little dog at the risk of his own ; but he never dreamed of him as a rival. There was no comparison between them. His own affairs, it is true, were in a very unprosperous condition. He had parted with half his patrimony in post-obits ; but still his father was a rich man and a peer, and he would one day stand in his shoes. Without being conceited he had considerable confidence—as indeed he had good reason to have—in his own personal attractions ; and if he had not made the way with Grace that he had hoped to make, he flattered himself that he had made some way ; she was certainly interested in him ; her manner was always gracious to him, and sometimes confidential—even tender. He had too much the start of her new acquaintance to fear him, even if the other should think of entering himself for the matrimonial stakes ; but no such notion occurred to him. He had no more chance than has a half-bred horse of winning the Derby. Sinclair, as he believed, and justly, had neither wealth nor position. His father had been, it was said, an unsuccessful merchant, and afterwards an adventurer, who had not succeeded even in that line. Nay, Sinclair had been an adventurer himself (though not in a bad sense), and took no pains to conceal the fact. He talked quite frankly to his companions of the shifts—not dishonourable, but still very disagreeable shifts—he had been sometimes put to in the course of his wanderings ; and though he had gathered more moss than the rolling-stone is generally credited with, he had only just enough of it to make him comfortable. He had been living for some time in London without a profession, and had become accepted in boating circles,

and that was about all that was known of
him. There would have seemed no reason to
Lord Cheribert, even had he thought about
the matter, which he did not, for his character
was singularly uncalculating, to object to the
introduction of Mr. Walter Sinclair to Elm
Place. There had been a time when the in-
trusion of a young gentleman with such antecedents into the family circle would have met
with serious opposition from Mr. Roscoe; but
it was not so now. Even if he had entertained
any apprehensions of one of the Miss Tremenheres falling in love with him, he would have
regarded the matter with philosophy, if not
with satisfaction, provided only—and this did
not seem probable—that the young man was
not of the Jewish faith. His keen eye had
perceived that the suit of the young lord was
not progressing with Miss Grace; perhaps the
presence of a rival might quicken his attentions, or perhaps the other might prove more
acceptable to the young lady. He had a

liberal mind as to her disposal in matrimony, and, as the nearest friend of the family, would have 'given her away' to anybody she fancied, or who fancied her, with a light (and lightened) heart.

What was also in Mr. Sinclair's favour, the two elder ladies—notwithstanding that it was their sister's dog he had saved, and that he had shown to her a somewhat marked preference after that proceeding—were not one whit jealous of him. Perhaps, with a modesty rather unusual even with their modest sex, they both thought him too young for them. They did not appear to expect any particular attentions at his hands, nor in the least to grudge those he paid to Grace.

It was natural enough, at first at all events, that he should pay them to her. The service he had rendered to her, though indirect, was a personal one, and it, of course, evoked her thanks, and what was more, her serious reproof. It was strange enough that to both these young men Grace should be placed, somehow, in the relation of a monitor; but so it was; and it put them in consequence on a certain familiar footing with her, which had she been a flirt she would have known how to use. The scolding of the young schoolmistress, though taken in good part, was not taken in the same way by her new friend as by her old one. She told him, as they were sitting on the lawn together after dinner, what had happened at Milton Weir before to Lord Cheribert's friend, and he drew a very serious face indeed.

'I had no idea of that,' he said; 'the spectacle of my absurd proceedings (swimming with a dog in one's mouth like something particularly foolish in heraldry) must have distressed you, I fear, from association.'

'It distressed me on your own account,' she answered; 'you might have been drowned like the other poor young fellow.'

'I don't suppose in my case it would have

mattered very much to anyone,' was his quiet rejoinder.

Here was another young man apparently without a mother or anybody else (except Grace) to take an interest in him; some girls would have thought themselves in great luck.

'How can you talk so wickedly, Mr. Sinclair!' she replied indignantly.

'Wickedly? Well, of course I'm wicked enough,' he answered, not with a drawl, but with that quaint hesitancy that belongs to many of the citizens of the Great Republic, and which he had probably picked up from them. 'I didn't say it might not have made some difference to *me*, but only that it would not have mattered to anyone else.'

'It would have mattered to your friends, I suppose,' she observed coldly.

'Yes, true; I suppose our fellows would have had to put off the match at Marlow next week, unless they could get another stroke.'

' You are a cynic, it seems, Mr. Sinclair.'

' Am I?' he smiled with evident satisfaction; 'I am so glad to be something. I am always so puzzled when men say to me, " What *are* you? Soldier, sailor, tinker, tailor, gentleman, apothecary, ploughboy, thief?" I have been almost all of them except the last; but just now I am nothing. In future, when that question is put to me, I shall know what to say—" My good sir, I am a cynic." '

The serious earnestness of his tone was such that his speech had no suspicion of flippancy, and far less of impertinence. Grace smiled in spite of herself.

' I am afraid you are an idle man, sir.'

' No, I don't admit that,' he answered gravely. ' I've worked—well, I don't suppose any of my friends among the men yonder know what work is—but I may say harder than most. And though I am still a young man I feel for the present I have had enough of work. I am enjoying myself just now—very much,' he added, with pleasant significance.

It was very difficult not to laugh at, or rather with, this young gentleman; he possessed the sort of good humour that is contagious.

'What I see now,' he continued, as if in explanation of his happy condition, and looking round at the others, who were engaged in mirthful conversation, ' is the first glimpse of home-life that has been vouchsafed to me for many a year.'

To his unaccustomed eye the comfort and quiet of the scene, as well as the demeanour of the actors, all seemingly at their ease, might well have given the impression of home; but to Grace, who by bitter and everyday experience knew how much of it was indeed acting, it seemed piteous that this brave and attractive young fellow should have rated it so high ; he must in truth, she thought, be without friends and belongings if the atmosphere of Elm Place had struck him as fragrant with the domestic virtues.

'I am glad that you are enjoying yourself,' she answered simply, 'but as to nobody caring whether you were drowned or not, I must say, in justice to Lord Cheribert, for one, that when he saw you were caught by those dreadful weeds, it was only by main force that he was restrained from jumping into the river and sharing what seemed to be your certain fate.'

'Was that so?' returned Sinclair, with a fine glow on his face. 'He may be assured that I shall not forget it. Lords must be made of better metal than folk on the other side of the Atlantic are apt to imagine.'

'This one at all events has a good deal of good about him, I think,' said Grace, with a grave smile.

'Really?' observed the young fellow, glancing at the subject of the conversation with an interest not unmingled with surprise. 'If you say so it doubtless must be so. And the other gentleman,' he gravely added, 'is he a good fellow too?'

The question was indeed a strange one, and, as it happened, even more embarrassing than it appeared to be; yet the visitor had asked it with the same coolness as he might have used had he been inquiring the age of Rip, who, as though conscious of his late obligation, had ensconced himself—not a little to Lord Cheribert's mortification—on the lap of the new-comer.

'Mr. Roscoe is a very old friend of our family,' replied Grace evasively.

'Really?' answered Sinclair, and again the word—evidently a favourite with him—had an intonation which seemed to suggest surprise. 'I am interested in him,' he went on more indifferently, 'because I once knew a man of the same name in Chicago.'

'Mr. Roscoe has a brother, I believe, in America. Do you see any resemblance in him to the gentleman you have in your mind?'

'None whatever; no, my man was very outspoken; "No one's enemy but his own," they said of him. Now this one, I should say, was of quite another sort.'

'It seems you are one of those gentlemen who pride themselves upon being a judge of character,' observed Grace, smiling.

'Well, yes, that is so. I don't know much about books; I have had little time, I am sorry to say, for reading; but about human nature—for a young one—I do claim to know a little. As soldier, sailor, tinker, tailor, gentleman, apothecary, and ploughboy I have seen a good deal of it.'

'Then a friend of mine would say—and you seem to be in doubt about a profession—you ought to make a good lawyer.'

'No, no; I particularly said that my callings did not include the whole of the proverbial list, but stopped at ploughboy.'

'If you mean to imply that thief and lawyer are synonymous, Mr. Sinclair,' put in

Grace with severity, 'I must be excused from agreeing with you.   The dearest friend I have now in the world, who is also the most honest of men, is a lawyer.'

'Really?' repeated the young fellow with ludicrous iteration.   'Well, let everyone speak as he finds.   The lawyers have been a little hard on me, it must be confessed!'   The speaker frowned mechanically as if at some remembrance of a wrong, and a harsh glitter came into his grey eyes, contrasting strangely with their usual softness.

'I should not have thought you were a person to bear malice,' observed Grace involuntarily.

'Well, no; I hope not on my own account,' he answered slowly; 'when I said the lawyers had been hard on me, I should have said on mine.   My father always laid his ruin at the door of one of them.   It is easier to forgive things done against oneself than against one's father, is it not?'

'No doubt,' assented Grace with unconscious sympathy. 'Is it long,' she added, moved by the association of ideas, 'since you lost your father, Mr. Sinclair?'

'Yes,' he replied, in a grave, slow way; 'I was but a boy when it happened. He was murdered by Indians.'

'Oh, how shocking!' ejaculated Grace.

The sound of her voice a little raised attracted the attention of the others, who were sitting in garden chairs only a few feet away, but still at a sufficient distance to prevent what the new-comer had said to her from becoming public property.

'What is the matter?' exclaimed Lord Cheribert. 'Not snakes, I do hope.'

There were snakes on the wooded hill which the imagination of his town-bred friends had gifted with the attributes of the cobra.

'No, not snakes,' answered Sinclair, smiling (for the joke had a meaning for him, though of another kind). 'To a Western man it would have seemed nothing, but I am afraid I have alarmed Miss Grace with speaking of an incident of the frontier.'

'It is most extraordinary,' observed Philippa, 'how the gentlemen who do us the honour of visiting Elm Place *will* regale us with horrible tales.'

'Nevertheless, let us hear it,' said Mr. Roscoe; 'I will try not to be very frightened.'

'No,' said Sinclair under his breath.

Perhaps it was only a mechanical utterance; but Grace, who noticed that the young fellow had turned pale, took it as an appeal for her to direct the conversation into another channel. It was only reasonable, she thought, since it was her ejaculation which had called attention to them. What had fallen from him quite naturally in private talk, and after due introduction, he might well object to make the subject of public comment.

'I really think we have had enough of

distressing incidents for to-day,' she said. Then in a lighter tone, ' Mr. Sinclair tells me that he knew a gentleman in America of your name, Mr. Roscoe. I wonder if it was your brother ? '

Mr. Roscoe, who had been lounging in his basket-chair, very much at his ease, suddenly drew himself up. ' Indeed ? ' he said with an indifference that rather contrasted with that movement. ' It is not very likely, for Richard has not mingled with his fellow-countrymen for years.'

' I have not seen him for years,' said Sinclair quietly ; ' but certainly his name was Richard. A tall man, rather loosely made, and of the same complexion as yourself, and a little older.'

' That seems to answer to what I remember of him,' said Mr. Roscoe, after a moment's hesitation ; ' but he is younger than I.'

' That is possible,' returned the other

thoughtfully. 'He was living a hard life—that, indeed, we all do out West,' he added hastily; 'but his passion was hunting, which out there means shooting. I know of few men who could maintain themselves so well by their rifles when game was scarce.'

'He must be your brother, Mr. Roscoe,' exclaimed Lord Cheribert, laughing. 'These sporting instincts run in a family.'

'It is generally a misfortune for the family when they do so,' observed Mr. Roscoe significantly. He was generally impervious to sarcasm, but on this occasion Lord Cheribert's sally seemed to have hit on a tender place.

'It was a misfortune for me in this case,' continued Sinclair, who understood, of course, the satire of neither speaker; 'for it was Richard Roscoe who persuaded my poor father to go to the plains, where he met with a miserable end—not that I blame your brother in the least, sir,' he added gently.

' He was a very frank and fearless fellow, and,
I am sure, a faithful friend.'

A sigh of reminiscence (or perhaps of
relief) here involuntarily broke from Mr.
Roscoe.

' I hope you have heard no ill-news of
your brother?' said the young man earnestly.

. ' No; not at all. He is in good health,
and in the last letter I had from him expressed his intention of returning to England.'

' Indeed? There is no man I wish more
to see,' said Sinclair eagerly. ' He would
have sought me out himself could he have
done so, I feel sure, though the tidings he
had to give me I know only too well, save in
their details.'

' How curious it all seems!' observed
Philippa, breaking the somewhat embarrassing silence; ' how strange that Mr. Sinclair
should be a friend of Mr. Roscoe's brother!
How small the world is!'

' Not the New World,' returned the new-comer gravely. 'Here in England we are accustomed to associate wide separation with the ocean. In America it is not so; though on the same continent, those who wish to meet are often deterred from doing so by thousands of miles of land-travel. Even that, of course, can be surmounted by those who have long purses; but that has, unfortunately, not been the case with my friends. No one knows what poverty is who has not been in a strange land cut off from all who are near and dear to him by the want of a few hundred dollars.'

Lord Cheribert and Grace involuntarily exchanged glances. 'You know what I told you,' his half-laughing look seemed to say, ' of the great convenience of ready-money.' ' You know what I told you,' her grave eyes seemed to say, ' of the selfishness of those who lavish great possessions upon their pleasures, when so many souls as well as bodies are in actual need.'

CHAPTER XXI

A DIFFICULT POSITION

THERE was fine weather on the river that year, which makes all the difference—except to fishermen. who are indifferent to the rain, or even like it—to those who live by the river.

Elm Place was a very bower of delight so far as nature could make it so. Unfortunately, human nature occasionally stepped in and stained the radiance of the sky.

Agnes and Philippa, for some reason which Grace could not comprehend, were at daggers drawn, or at all events very loosely sheathed. They no longer agreed even in abusing their dead father; it was a topic not indeed exhausted, but, as it seemed, in abeyance. Mr. Roscoe was their only bond of union; his personal influence was always exerted in favour of peace, but he had the greatest difficulty in enforcing it. They each appealed to him, against one another: but Philippa the most urgently. 'Agnes' conduct, Edward,' she would say to him, 'is becoming intolerable; not an hour goes by in which she does not insult me by words or gesture.'

'How can you be so foolish!' he would reply contemptuously. 'What does it really matter? You can surely afford to bear with her infirmities.'

'You speak of them as if they were natural weaknesses, the infirmities of age.'

'Well, perhaps they are,' he answered with a smile; and neither the words nor the smile displeased her. 'You must be patient, Philippa; you are not the only person who has to suffer. To quarrel with your sister just now would be your ruin. You can always quarrel, and there are other matters which are more pressing.   It is most important to get Grace off our hands before anything else is done.'

'That is not so easy as you predicted. She likes Lord Cheribert, but not well enough to marry him.   Her liking for him does not grow.'

'Then let her take up with Sinclair.'

'Take up, indeed!   That shows the value you place on a woman's love,' she exclaimed bitterly.

'Nay, nay, you know better than that,' he replied softly.   'The phrase was a coarse one, I admit; but seriously it seems to me that Grace *is* leaning towards this young fellow at an acuter angle, as it were, than she leaned to the other.   So long as she falls into the arms of one of them, it is no matter which.'

'How hard you are, Edward!   I am sometimes tempted to think that everything is a matter of calculation with you; that love is worth nothing in your eyes.'

'Not even a risk?' he put in gravely.

'I don't say that,' she continued less vehemently. 'But it seems to be not worth a loss.'

'A loss? You speak as if the matter were one in my eyes in which love was in one scale and money in the other, and that the latter weighed down the former. You *know* that that is not the case, Philippa.'

'I know that I am a very miserable woman,' she answered with a sob.

'How unreasonable you are!' he said reprovingly; 'it is not two months ago that, on a certain occasion, when your imprudence—nay, and mine, too, I confess it—was, you remember, almost the cause of our undoing——'

'Don't speak of it,' she broke in, in terrified accents. 'Remember it? Can I ever forget it?'

'And yet, to hear you now, one would think you had forgotten it. I say that when that happened you solemnly promised me it should be the last of our risks; a lesson you would lay to heart, and never cease to remember ; that henceforth my motto should be " Patience," and yours should be " Trust." '

'I do trust you,' she answered in a voice half choked by tears, ' and in more ways than one, as you well know ; but I did think that when—when our circumstances altered there would be no need for patience.'

'So did I,' was the quiet rejoinder. ' Again you speak, Philippa, as if you were the only sufferer. I say I thought so too ; and who would not have thought so?' His face was white with passion, and he clenched his hands as though in recollection of some grievous wrong. 'We have been cruelly treated, you and I: but it cannot last for ever. If our freedom does not come by one way, it will come by another. It is for that that I have been waiting ; though, hitherto, it is true, the Fates have been against us. On Grace's marriage, remember, we should have much more to work with.'

'More money? What do we want with money?' she inquired passionately. 'I hate the very name of money.'

'Still it is a necessary evil,' he answeréd dryly. 'You do not wish your sister Agnes to inherit the whole of your father's property, I suppose? You would not be obliged to her for the scraps she might throw to you out of her abundance. You would not like to be patronised by her as a poor relation?'

'I should not indeed,' she answered vehemently ; the fire in her eyes, the flush on her cheek, the impatient beat of her foot upon the ground, showed how little she would like it.

'Then let Trust and Patience be our mottoes for a little longer. Everything comes to them who wait.'

Thus, time after time, did Edward Roscoe stave off the question, 'How long is this to last?' from Philippa Tremenhere. It was a difficult task, but not so difficult as to answer the same inquiry from her elder sister.

Agnes was far bolder than Philippa, because her position, as she thought, was assured. She could hardly call Philippa a chit of a girl, but she regarded her absurd attachment for Mr. Roscoe much as if she were one. It was a mere foolish fancy, which one word of outspeaking on her own part would burst like the pricking of a bubble; but unhappily it was impossible to speak it.

'I am sick and tired, Edward, of Philippa's silly fluttering about you like a moth about a candle,' she would say, with angry impatience.

'And do you suppose *I* am not sick and tired of it too?' would be his bitter rejoinder. 'You only suffer from it, remember, at second hand.'

'That is all nonsense,' she replied sharply; 'a man never dislikes seeing a woman make a fool of herself for his sake; but it drives the woman who loves him to distraction.'

'I am ashamed to hear you say so, Agnes. You should have more self-restraint—I had almost said self-respect—if not for your sake, for mine.'

'It is for neither of our sakes, sir, that you use such arguments,' she answered, hardly, 'but merely for the desire of gain.'

Agnes Tremenhere's temper was naturally what is termed 'short,' and for the moment she had lost it; otherwise she would hardly have ventured to utter such a home truth to the only man on earth of whom she stood in fear. The effect of it recalled her to her senses, though what she thought its consequence was far less serious than it really was. Mr. Roscoe turned his back upon her, not as she imagined in high offence, but to conceal the expression of unquench-able hate which he knew, despite his powers of self-control, his face would reveal to her.

If he could have killed her by a look, he would have looked at her. Nothing, save that it was a quotation from Shakspeare, could excuse the hiss that passed through his teeth, 'Hell cat!' Fortunately it was uttered as 'an aside,' but the involuntary movement of the muscles of his back—the unmistakable index of extreme fear or rage —did not escape her attention.

'I did not mean that, Edward,' she exclaimed hurriedly. 'I did not know what I was saying!'

'I hope not,' was the pained reply. He had turned round now, and was regarding her with reproachful amazement, such as some domestic pet, unconscious of wrong-doing, might exhibit when struck by its mistress.

'Heaven forbid that I should grudge you,' she continued tenderly, 'whatever you may need in that way! But you set too great a store on it. What is wealth compared with happiness!'

'True, but why should it not be combined with happiness?' he replied persuasively. 'There are few men worthy of you, Agnes; there is no man, deserving to be called a man, who for the sake of such happiness as you speak of would be your ruin.'

'It is not a question of ruin,' she answered doggedly. She had come to herself as quickly as he had come to what he wished her to believe was *himself*.

'It is a question, however, of whether you should recklessly give up a huge fortune to swell that which Philippa already possesses. We must have patience, Agnes.'

'That is a text from which you are always preaching; you promised me that at a certain time there should be an end of that sermon; and the time is past, and still I find you preaching.'

'Because the tree does not bring forth its expected fruit, that is no reason why we should curse the tree. I mean you to have what in common justice should be your own, but it cannot be done in a day. If I did what you wish you would not thank me for it, though you think you would. How would you endure to live on a few hundreds a year, while Philippa had her tens of thousands?'

'She would not be happy,' she answered gravely.

'Yes, that is the key of it all,' he replied contemptuously. 'You wish me to sell your rightful inheritance for a mess of pottage— the satisfaction of contemplating the humiliation and disappointment of your sister. You may see that yet, but it must be from a standpoint above her and not below. I must be admitted to have a clearer view of this matter than you, Agnes; I am not blinded by prejudice.'

'So it seems,' she replied bitterly.

'Thank you. I hope that is another of the things which you say without knowing what you say. It is idle to argue with you

while you are in this state. Let us go in.'
They were walking on what was called 'the camp shed'—the terrace paved with wood, at the foot of the lawn, and overhanging the river. He made a movement as though he would go up to the house, but she clutched his arm.

'Stay—I am ready to listen to reason. What would you have me do?'

'Have patience. That is all that is left for us both, for the present. Time is on our side, and fighting in our favour. Grace is falling in love with Walter Sinclair.'

'It is very foolish of her; Lord Cheribert would be far the better match.'

'No doubt; but women *are* foolish. However, so far as we are concerned, the one is as good as the other. She has the same contempt for riches that you have persuaded yourself you entertain; but in her case it is genuine. She will marry, and perhaps be happy on a little, while we reap the fruits of her moderation. That will be one obstacle removed from our path.'

' And Philippa?'

' Well, of course that will be more difficult. If it were anyone else I should propose a compromise.'

'I don't understand you.' She spoke with something more than gravity; with all her faults Agnes Tremenhere was an honest woman, and though she professed to be ignorant of his meaning, it was not so.

'Do you think that I propose to rob your sister?' he returned sharply. The flush upon his cheek was genuine enough, but it was not caused by virtuous indignation, as she imagined; he was furious at her scruples, or rather at his having proposed to her a shameful course of action which it was now clear to him she would have nothing to do with; he had almost shown his hand to her in vain.

She was frightened at his vehemence, as

he had intended her to be; but she was still in doubt—as she well might be—as to the motive of the compromise, since it seemed it was not a proposal to obtain money under false pretences.

'What I was going to say was, that if circumstances had been different it would have been possible for you all three to have combined together to make the iniquitous provisions of your father's will null and void. There would have been no harm in that, I suppose. Justice, if not law, would have been on our side in a plan, for instance, whereby you all three married and yet by mutual agreement kept your own.'

She nodded in acquiescence; then added, with a sigh, 'But then there is Philippa.'

'Just so; with her—as I was about to say when you interrupted me so very un-necessarily—no compromise is possible.'

'It is most shameful that it should be so,' exclaimed Agnes passionately.

'Still so it is. Heaven is my witness that I don't care two straws about her; but I own that I am afraid of her. A jealous woman—whether she has any right to be so or not—is a very dangerous enemy.'

Who looked at Agnes Tremenhere at that moment could have no doubt of the fact. Her freckled face was livid, her lips white, with jealous hate.

'Let the shameful creature do her worst!' she cried.

'By all means; but not to *us*,' he answered quietly. 'She will find me a match for her, in one sense at all events. Listen to me. When Grace is married, it is probable that things will be even worse at home than they are; it is one of those cases where things must be worse before they are better. Philippa and you will have to part.'

She looked up at him with a glow of joy. 'I see; but not you and I, Edward?'

'Or, if we do, it will be only for a little

time, and in order to be united for ever.
What we must do is to persuade Mrs. Linden
to take her.'

'She will never do that; you would have
to get Philippa's consent to go to her. They
hate one another.'

'You leave that to me,' he answered con-
fidently, taking her hand in his and tenderly
stroking it.

'They will see us from the house,' she
murmured apprehensively, but without with-
drawing her hand. His touch was delightful
to her; it had the soothing charm of the
'pass' of the mesmerist; and it was so very,
very seldom that he allowed himself even so
small a privilege.

'Let them,' he answered defiantly. Then,
dropping her fingers with a sigh, he added,
'No, you are right, Agnes; we cannot be too
prudent. I have a plan in my head, but it
must ripen. In the meantime, encourage
Sinclair, if you think he is the surest card to

play. He is a fisherman; ask him to come up to Cumberland next month and try the Rill.'

'But Lord Cheribert tells me he is coming.

'No matter; let them both come. Perhaps Philippa will take the rejected one,' and he laughed softly.

But Agnes gave no answering smile; it was a subject that had no touch of humour for her, though she liked *his* laughing.

'We must keep her in good humour as well as we can,' he went on cheerfully; 'you must not mind my being civil to her. It will be all the worse for her in the end.'

That was naturally a subject for congratulation, but Agnes Tremenhere's face did not display it; she did not like the prospect of those occasional civilities.

'When you talk to me, Edward,' she said piteously, 'I always feel for the time persuaded; but when you are not talking to me —and, above all, when you are talking to *her*

—I am a very miserable woman. I can't bear it much longer ; I can't, indeed.'

'*Much* longer it will not be necessary to bear it, Agnes,' he answered gravely ; 'once more I say to you, have patience. It is five o'clock ; they are all coming down from the hill yonder. Go in and make the tea.'

She left him, and he entered an arbour at the extremity of the camp shed and sat down. His face was pale, and the dew stood upon his forehead. He had had a very trying time with her, but that was not the reason of his emotion, or why he trembled in every limb. Nor was it the plan he had told her he was devising for ridding them of Philippa ; for in truth he had had no plan : that was but a device for gaining time. It was only a thought that had crossed his mind during his late interview—at the moment when he had turned his back upon his companion—and which now that he was left alone came back to him ; but it was a very terrible thought, born of hate and rage, and nourished by disappointment and despair ; it shook his very soul within him.

He lit a cigar, but the gentle weed brought none of its wonted dreams and oblivious consolations ; if it brought dreams at all, they were nightmares, and made his own society so intolerable that after a whiff or two he flung the cigar into the river, and sought the society of his fellow-creatures, in order to forget them. But he did not forget them even then ; the dreadful thought which had moved him so was an unbidden guest at that five-o'clock tea.

CHAPTER XXII

A HANDSOME OFFER

WHEN people have nothing serious to do love-making goes on apace, which is one of the reasons why idle folks are always getting into mischief. Lord Cheribert, as it will have been concluded, was already deeply smitten by Grace, and though Walter Sinclair had started so long behind him he had made up for lost time, and was soon as much in love as he. The difference of social position, which, though he did not acknowledge it to himself, made the young lord so easy in his mind as regarded his possible rival, did not afflict Walter one whit. In this respect his very deficiencies were to his advantage; he was naturally far from conceited, but the manner of his bringing up, and the unconventional life he had led, prevented his recognising his inferiority.

In his view one man was as good as another until the other had shown himself the better man. In the part of the world where he had been living rank had not been much thought of, for the simple reason that it did not exist; and wealth, though more highly considered (for what it procured, not for itself), was transitory. A man made his pile in a few months, and often lost it again in the same number of hours. Lord Cheriberts, without the Lord, he had often met with, who were ready to lay their bottom dollar, or their top one, upon any event, so that *that* side of the young nobleman's character was quite intelligible to him. He looked upon it with great charity, but also some contempt, and thought it a pity so good a fellow should have made such a fool of himself. For as to other matters he admired him, though he could scarcely say for what. It was the first time he had experienced, in a man, the charm of manner, and he was attracted by it none the less because it showed itself in a rival. In that respect he at once admitted the other's superiority, but in that alone.

In his relations with Grace, though he did not conceal from himself that he loved her, his position was entirely different; he was humility itself; and this also was more owing to his upbringing than to his nature, which was one of practical common-sense. In the Wild West, and even in the West where it is not so wild, there is an admiration for the female more in proportion to her rarity than her deserts; the most commonplace girl is a heroine, and women of the earth, earthy, are reckoned goddesses. The mistake is highly creditable to a community in which tender-ness and refinement are not the leading features, and, though in individual cases it is sometimes disastrous, has on the whole a civilising effect. Moreover, what is very curious, though it makes rough men gentle in their relations with the other sex, it does not make them shy. The knowledge, perhaps, that they may be called upon at any moment to act as their protectors—a term in the Old World which has, alas! changed its meaning —induces a certain familiarity, which has at the same time no tinge of disrespect. No one could accuse Walter Sinclair of shyness; he had a perfect self-possession that Mr. Roscoe mistook for 'cheek,' but, the ladies well understood, was nothing of the kind; he showed it when conversing with Grace, as with everybody else, but his respect for her was reverential. There was nothing to be found fault with in Lord Cheribert as to that (and considering what *his* upbringing had been, it was proof indeed of his honest nature), but the difference between them in this matter was very great. Where the young nobleman felt his unworthiness was in his fallen fortunes, or at deepest in the folly that had destroyed them; whereas Sinclair bowed before her as to a shrine of Purity which he trembled to approach even with his shoes off. Women in England are slow to understand this position of affairs, nor is it of much consequence, since it so seldom takes place. The two young fellows became great friends, but we may be sure they never talked of these matters.

The Miss Tremenheres had almost come to an end of their tenancy at Elm Place when Mr. Allerton paid them a visit; it was natural enough that he should do so, since he would have no other opportunity, as they were not to return to town before going to Cumberland; but, as a matter of fact, this was only the secondary object of his coming. He wanted to see Lord Cheribert on business matters, and he was much pleased, and not at all surprised, to find him where he was. The gentlemen of course all lodged at Milton, but they boarded over the way. The lawyer smiled when he discovered how very much at home the young nobleman made himself there, and was not at all alarmed at finding Sinclair doing the like. He took his lordship's view as regarded any danger to be apprehended from him as a possible rival in Grace's affections, only more so.

To a family solicitor, above all other people in the world, the claims of birth and wealth (for the two must be combined; it is no use your being descended from Hengist if you have but 300*l.* a year) seem overwhelming, even in courtship. The ladies who are his clients, however young and innocent they may be of the world's ways, have generally an instinct for eligibility. They may fall in love, and even at first sight, like Mary Jane and Jemima Anne, but not without having some previous knowledge of the position and property of their enslaver. The majority of these possible heroes are out of the question before they can make their first observation about Ascot or Mr. Irving.

A certain atmosphere, not necessarily of property but of appropriateness, surrounds the person of such heiresses as divinity is said to hedge a king. Cases have been known, of course, where the merest adventurers have broken through it and carried off their prize, but the incident is rare ; moreover, though the character of Walter Sinclair was by no means easy for a man like Mr. Allerton to read, it was clear to him that he was no adventurer, at all events in the ordinary sense. He had no swagger, no pretence of any kind ; he was not particularly polite ; he looked you straight in the face when he spoke to you, and when he spoke of his belongings he was anything but boastful. His father, to judge by his own account of him, had been far from prosperous ; beyond that point in his genealogy, either from charity or want of knowledge, he forbore to speak ; and it was the lawyer's experience that your adventurer can never avoid references to his grandfather. Moreover, Sinclair referred to his own past as having been neither successful nor satisfactory, which in a young gentleman who had at five-and-twenty years of age apparently made enough money to live upon for the rest of his days, was certainly a proof of modesty.

Still Mr. Allerton gave more attention to the young fellow than he would have done had he met him only in male society, and what he saw of him he liked, with one exception. He did not like the respect he showed to Mr. Edward Roscoe. The lawyer, of course, was prejudiced against that gentleman ; but even allowing for that, it was certainly strange that an honest young fellow such as Sinclair appeared to be, and also of great independence of character, should take to him at all. At first, indeed, this circumstance awoke grave suspicions in Mr. Allerton. He knew that Roscoe wanted Grace to marry ; and if she could be married to some creature of his own instead of Lord Cheribert, who was now altogether removed from his influence, it would obviously be to his advantage; moreover, he thought he detected a willingness on the part of Roscoe to play into Sinclair's hands. If there was really any agreement, tacit or otherwise, between the two men, it would be a very serious matter. This unworthy suspicion, it is only due to the lawyer's honest heart, as well as to his sagacity, to say, did not last long; and though the problem why Sinclair was so civil to Roscoe still puzzled him, it ceased to have much importance.

Lord Cheribert's affairs were at all events much more pressing. It is a drawback to a man of financial genius like the late Mr. Joseph Tremenhere, or at all events a drawback to his clients, that his excessive skill in the management of affairs, and the self-confidence born of it, causes him to take every thread in his own hands, and trust little or nothing to others; this works well enough while he is alive to hold the threads—and therefore answers his purpose with sufficient completeness—but when he dies his multifarious operations often present a tangled web to those who come after him.

The knots by which Josh had secured his own interests were neat enough, but the ramifications of his clients' affairs were numerous and intricate. In Lord Cheribert's case they were particularly so, because of his own recklessness and contempt for business transactions. It is distressing to a lawyer when he asks a client in whom he feels a personal interest, 'Is this your signature, my lord?' to be answered, 'It looks like it, but I have not the faintest remembrance of ever having put it there.'

Lord Cheribert had no recollection of any debt that wasn't a bet, which greatly impeded the settlement of his affairs. Sundry creditors were pressing him with their little accounts, and showing a strong disinclination to 'let them run,' even to the date when, as all the world now knew, Lord Morella was to come forward and show that a father had his duties as well as his privileges. In the aggregate these debts came to a large sum, though they sank into almost insignificance compared with the obligations due to the Tremenhere estate; those, however, we may be sure, were well secured, and the family could afford to wait; the family, indeed, knew nothing about them; it was not thought necessary by Mr. Allerton to go into such details with the ladies, and Mr. Roscoe, though of course he knew all about them, had likewise abstained from communicating them. It was quite sufficient for the purposes of both those gentlemen that Lord Cheribert should know the facts.

It would no doubt have distressed the ladies to feel that their guest was their debtor, and would have made their relations with him not a little embarrassing; whereas it was the lawyer's secret hope that his client would see for himself how extremely convenient it would be to pay off $33\frac{1}{3}$ per cent. of his obligations by a matrimonial union with one of the fair creditors; if he had thought of it the probability is, the effect would have been exactly the reverse of what was intended; but, as a matter of fact, the circumstance never occurred to him; Lord Cheribert never thought of his creditors.

Some of them, however, as has been said, thought a good deal of him (though not in an appreciatory sense), and were making themselves very unpleasant. Lord Morella could have stopped them with a word, but that word he would not speak till his son had given up his evil ways for good and all. He had promised to do so, as we know, at a certain date; but until that day arrived his father declined to have anything to do with him. His paternal affection was ready laid, like a housemaid's fire, but he positively declined to apply the match to it till after the 14th proximo, when his son's last steeplechase was to come off. The Earl had an immense reputation for 'determination of character,' and it was inherited by his son and heir, though in him he described it as the obstinacy of a pig. He would not advance a shilling to help him, nor permit his lawyer to advance one; and, on the other hand, the young man would not pay forfeit for the race in question, though the old lord would have gladly laid down the money twenty times over. Matters had come, in short, to a deadlock, and the worst of it was that the circumstances greatly militated against the genuineness of the promised re-conciliation between father and son : you can't hold over affection like an accommodation bill, nor postpone filial love to a particular date in the calendar; they are apt to grow cool in the meantime.

The lawyer had at least as much tact as members of his profession usually possess, and

had endeavoured to conciliate both sides—
though he would have much preferred to
knock their heads together—but his efforts
were in vain; he began to fear that a public
scandal could hardly be averted, and if that
took place Lord Cheribert's chance with Grace
would be seriously endangered; it was difficult to hint to him of this peril, and if it had
been done he would probably have thought
little of it, he was himself so used to public
scandals.

On the matter of his debts, indeed, he was
—with men—entirely without reticence, and
he not a little disconcerted the good lawyer
by speaking of them in the smoking-room at
Elm Place with his usual frankness.

'What *does* it matter?' he said, when re-
proached by Mr. Allerton for his imprudence.
'*You* know all about them, Roscoe knows all
about them; and to Sinclair, who, though an
excellent fellow himself, has probably been
witness to half the crimes in the calendar and

some outside it, the fact of a man's being in a hole as regards money matters can appear nothing very serious. Any talk of that kind must be to him like a description of a day with the rabbits on the hill, after a tiger-hunt; there is not enough sport in it to attract his attention.'

The lawyer smiled; he was much too wise to press the point, or any point that was not absolutely essential, on 'such a cat-a-mountain of a client'; but he thought it possible that the financial embarrassments of Lord Cheribert might have some attraction for Mr. Sinclair notwithstanding their want of dramatic interest. Nor, as it turned out, was he mistaken.

On the morning after the conversation in the smoking-room, Mr. Allerton, who was an early riser, found Sinclair on the lawn at Milton before breakfast, with a short black pipe in his mouth of the most reprehensible appearance.

'It's a bad habit, I know,' said that young gentleman, noting the look which the lawyer bestowed upon his clay idol, ' but our fellows breakfast late here, and there's nothing like tobacco for staying the appetite.'

'So I should think,' returned the lawyer dryly ; ' if I was to smoke a pipe before breakfast, I should never eat anything all day.'

' It does not interfere in that way with me at all, as you will see at breakfast-time,' answered the young fellow, laughing, ' and there have been days when want of appetite was not so much my difficulty as the want of anything to eat ; then a pipe is a boon indeed.'

' Things have been as bad as that with you, have they ?' replied the lawyer ; he rather liked his new acquaintance (save for that inexplicable civility of his to Roscoe), and was not unwilling to hear something of his past ; it might come under the head of useful knowledge.

' Yes ; one does not always get fresh eggs

in the morning out West, and claret-cup '—he pointed to the place across the river where that compound was exceedingly well made, as they both knew—' is unknown at the diggings.'

' At the diggings ? You were there, were you ? I hope you made your pile.'

' I don't look like that, do I ? I hope not.'

The other did not understand what he meant, but saw no necessity to inquire ; he was not in search of sentiments but facts. Experience had taught him not to interrupt when his object was to obtain information. You may generally trust a man who is talking about himself to proceed with that interesting subject.

' Yes, I was the man who first found gold at One Tree Hill.'

The lawyer nodded, as if he was as conversant with that locality as with Shooter's Hill or Primrose Hill.

'There were three of us,' continued the young fellow, in a tone of a reminiscence, and with that far-off look in his eyes which the ladies had noticed; 'we had but ten dollars amongst us, but it was not a place to spend much money in; not a hut within ten miles, and the nearest drinking-bar a long day's journey from us. I wish to heaven,' he added with vehemence, 'it had been further still.'

He paused; an observation seemed to be expected.

'Drink must be a great temptation in those out-of-the-way places,' hazarded the lawyer.

'Not to *me*, sir,' was the haughty rejoinder. 'There is no man living who has ever seen Walter Sinclair drunk.' Had Lord Cheribert been present it is possible he would have suggested that there might be more reasons than one for that; there was a certain solemnity in the young man's assertion that might well have provoked raillery; but it did not do so with Mr. Allerton. He understood that the conditions of existence of which the other was speaking were very different from his present ones, and that his boast was not only genuine but had a justification. ' However, better men than I have given way to liquor,' continued Sinclair modestly, ' and it is easy to resist what has no attractions for one.'

' It must be a great experience, that first finding of gold,' remarked the lawyer tentatively, like a huntsman casting for the scent.

The young man nodded assentingly. ' Yes. For the moment it appears as if one had found everything. To penniless men like us it seemed like heaven itself. The first nugget might be the last, of course, but it might also be wealth beyond the dreams of avarice. Some men think of the gold itself; others, of what they will do with it. I had at that time a use for wealth, and my discovery filled me with delirious joy. Our first act was to solemnly swear that we would keep the matter secret from our fellow-creatures. We worked like galley-slaves, but for a rate of pay that would have satisfied a prime minister. We had hit on a very rich lode. On the fourth day one of the two men who were prospecting with me disappeared. The other when he missed him uttered the most frantic execrations. " What is the matter? " I said. " Why should Dick have come to harm? " " Harm! " he answered, " I wish he had a bullet through his brain! He will bring harm to *us*. The mad fool is off to the drinking-bar." " But he will come back again, I suppose? " " Yes, but with five thousand men to rob us of our rights." He judged only too well. The doting wretch, having money in his pocket, or the equivalent of it, could not resist the demon for a dram ; once in liquor, he began of course to boast of the new gold-diggings, and the morning of the third day saw a cloud of miners coming like locusts over the hill. They behaved fairly enough, and gave us the first choice of claim as discoverers. We elected to stay on our patch, and in a fortnight there was not another ounce of gold to be got in it, though we worked as hard as ever. Other men were more lucky, and made great fortunes; nor, indeed, had I any right to complain, since in that one month I made enough to keep me, I hope, and something over, for the remainder of my days.'

'A golden month, indeed,' observed the lawyer.

'Yet the vilest one man ever passed,' answered the other vehemently. 'Greed is unpleasant enough to look upon in any shape, but as you see it naked and unashamed in a goldfield it is loathsome indeed. I should not have troubled you with such a story at all, Mr. Allerton, but for a reason: if it had not been told, you might have said to yourself, "This rolling-stone has probably gathered no moss," and you would have been disinclined to believe in my solvency.'

'Why should you say that?' said the lawyer, smiling. He meant of course to be complimentary; to imply that no suspicion of his companion's want of means had ever entered his mind; but the other took him *au pied de la lettre.*

'Well, for this reason. I was obliged to overhear Lord Cheribert's talk last night about his private affairs. It seems there is some hitch about the immediate settlement of certain debts, which may cause him some embarrassment: I don't understand the matter, but I wish to say that 5,000*l.* or so of what I possess is ready to my hand, and very much at his service.'

'Do I understand that you offer to lend Lord Cheribert 5,000*l.* on his note of hand?'

'Certainly; or without it.'

It was a matter of professional principle with Mr. Allerton never to be surprised at anything, but this proposition fairly staggered him. It was evident that the man who made it was no fool, and must therefore very well comprehend that his proposition if carried into effect would do away with the one advantage he possessed over his rival (if such, as the lawyer suspected, Lord Cheribert was) in being free from financial embarrassment ; nay, he must be aware, from what had passed in the smoking-room, that the existence of these debts of his lordship's threatened him with public exposure, which must be prejudicial indeed to any matrimonial project. Yet here was this young fellow actually offering to supply his rival with the sinews of war —and love. As a matter of fact, the offer could not be accepted, and would be utterly insufficient if it was. Mr. Allerton, of course, could have raised any amount of money to supply the young lord's temporary needs ; but this Lord Morella had positively forbidden him to do.

The young lord could not procure the sum required on his own security, and his father hoped to use his helplessness as a lever to effect his own object, namely, Lord Cheribert's immediate retirement from the turf. To have taken Sinclair's money (even had it been sufficient) would have been to break his word to the old lord, which Mr. Allerton was incapable of doing; but nothing of this was, of course, known to Sinclair, and the thought of the young man's unselfish generosity moved the old lawyer very much.

'You are a capital fellow, Sinclair,' he exclaimed, ' and I thank you five thousand times on behalf of my young friend and client; but your offer, liberal as it is, is useless to him; I am sorry and ashamed to say it would be a mere drop in the ocean.'

' I am sorry,' observed the other gravely. ' Perhaps I ought to have known as much. I hope,' he added, with a quick flush, ' that you do not think I did know it, Mr. Allerton ?'

' I am quite sure you did not. Your offer, I am convinced, was as genuine as it was generous. Will you gratify a curiosity that is not mere inquisitiveness and tell me why you made it?'

'Well, it is hardly worth talking about, and especially since it has come to nothing; but the fact is, even if I had been so fortunate as to help Lord Cheribert out of a tight place, the obligation would still have been on my side. When *I* was in a tight place in trouble with the weeds down yonder'—and he pointed over his shoulder in the direction of Milton lasher—'it was all they could do, I have been told, to prevent Lord Cheribert coming to drown with me. He did kick off his shoes to do it. One doesn't forget a thing like that, you know.'

'But you had done the same, it seems, for a dog?'

'I? That was very different. I was used to taking my life in my hand, as a thing not especially valuable. Don't mistake me for one of the mock-modest ones; I think myself every bit as good as his lordship, or any other lord in the land. But that is not *his* view, I reckon. Here was a young fellow who thought a huge lot of himself, and of whom other people thought more, ready to fling his all away on the off-chance of saving a mere loafer, a nobody—of course you will not tell him one word of this.'

'Of course not : here's my hand upon it. And now, Mr. Sinclair, if I have not exhausted your patience, just one question more. What is the obligation that binds you to Mr. Roscoe ? He didn't kick off *his* shoes, I'll be sworn.'

'I am under no obligation to Mr. Roscoe.'

'No, but you think you are ; at all events you behave as if you were. Come : you must not be angry with an old fellow who has nothing but your good at heart, or, what will weigh with you more, the good of another whom you esteem, I think. I say again it is not mere inquisitiveness that makes me put

the question. Why do you pay such defe-
rence to Mr. Roscoe ? '

' He not being one of my own sort at all,
as you would seem to say,' returned the young
man, smiling. ' Well, I don't know that he is.
But he has a brother—Dick—who was one of
the firmest friends (though not a very lucky
one) that my poor father ever had ; and for
his sake I can't help leaning toward Mr.
Edward perhaps a trifle more than he deserves
—Dick is coming home this autumn, I am
glad to hear.'

' Indeed ? ' was the dry rejoinder. ' Well,
in the meantime, my dear Mr. Sinclair, take
my advice, and when leaning towards Mr.
Edward be very careful not to lean *on* him,
for he's not the kind of prop that stands a
strain. Come, let us go in to breakfast.'

CHAPTER XXIII

GOOD ADVICE

It was curious, since Walter Sinclair was but a chance visitor of the Tremenheres, with whom their acquaintance would probably not at most outlast their occupancy of Elm Place, that Mr. Allerton should have troubled himself to give that word of warning to the young fellow. His motives for so doing were mixed, and perhaps not recognised even by himself. He had not only a well-grounded distrust but a very cordial dislike of Mr. Roscoe, which would have prompted him to set anyone on his guard whom he perceived to be subject to that gentleman's influence. But he had also begun to entertain a liking for Sinclair, almost in despite of himself.

Home-trained young gentlemen who, instead of becoming clerks to respectable solicitors, or embracing other decent professions in their own country, emigrated to uncivilised climes and tried their luck in goldfields, were not, as a rule, at all to his taste. He had, as we know, even entertained the suspicion that this young man had been a creature of Roscoe himself, and at all events felt it to be a mistake that a person of his condition had been allowed to attain a familiar footing with such a family as the Tremenheres. Now he certainly thought differently upon these points. There was a frankness about the young man that disarmed his doubts; and an independence of character that no longer seemed to him the impudence of the adventurer.

The generosity of his late offer was something altogether out of the lawyer's experience, and made a deep impression on him. For a moment it had struck him that though Sinclair had imposed silence about it to Lord

Cheribert he might not have been as unwilling for Grace to hear of it; but that he dismissed from his mind as an unworthy suspicion. He felt that Sinclair was incapable of such a method of recommending himself; while at the same time the action convinced him that he had no serious intention of becoming her suitor: it would in that case have been putting weapons into the hand of an adversary which neither gratitude nor chivalry demanded—a mere Quixotic act. Assured, therefore, that there was no danger of that kind to be apprehended, Mr. Allerton allowed his liking for the young fellow to have free course. He praised him to Grace, and he praised him to Lord Cheribert, and was pleased to find that they both shared his good opinion of him.

With the elder Miss Tremenheres Sinclair also appeared to be a favourite; Mr. Roscoe —but this was not placed to the credit side of the young man's account—treated him with marked civility. To any outsider, indeed, like Sinclair himself, who knew nothing of Agnes and Philippa as volcanoes, whose eruption was suppressed with difficulty by a master hand, the company at Elm Place seemed a very pleasant one, who had little to think about beyond amusement, and making themselves agreeable.

At the best, however, it was evident it was but a holiday party.

'You will miss your guests when you leave Elm Place,' said Mr. Allerton to Miss Agnes; 'Cumberland will seem just a little *triste* at first, I fear.'

'Lord Cheribert has promised to look in upon us; he has taken rooms at the " Angler's Rest " for the fishing.'

'Indeed!' This was news to Mr. Allerton, and good news. 'That will be very pleasant both for him and for you.'

'And Mr. Sinclair talks of coming too, upon the same errand.'

'Indeed!' He used the same word, but with a very different intonation. Matters, then, were much more serious in that quarter than he had anticipated. Sinclair had told him, when he had remonstrated with him in a paternal way on having no profession, that he rather thought of becoming a civil engineer. But the vicinity of Halswater Hall was hardly suitable for the prosecution of that design. He could not bring himself to believe that the young fellow could think of entering the lists against Lord Cheribert; but the circumstance determined him to speak a word or two with his client. The more he thought of the young lord's difficulties the more he felt convinced that a union with Grace was the best and quickest way out of them, supposing only that her father's will could be set aside—a matter which, though he could not well move in it himself, he felt could be accomplished by mutual agreement. It was curious, considering his own strong religious convictions, that Grace's faith did not present an insurmountable obstacle; but she was certainly not strongly attached to her creed ; and it is observable that whereas religious persons exceedingly resent any apostasy from their own communion, they think it the most natural thing in the world that others should exchange theirs for it.

So, when he and his client were strolling in the woods one day, he suddenly observed to him—it must be confessed, rather *à propos des bottes*, but the other, as he justly guessed, by design, never gave him the least chance of alluding to the subject—'Well, I hope Miss Grace is as great a favourite of yours as she is of mine, Cheribert.'

'How can you ask such a question ? ' was the unexpected rejoinder, delivered in the driest of tones. ' Miss Grace is a favourite with everybody.'

' Well, that is one of the reasons why I did ask it,' returned the lawyer. He was piqued by the young man's unwillingness to confide in him, and also irritated by the indifference he had all along exhibited to the dangerous condition of his affairs. 'It is really time, Cheribert, that you took things more seriously. I had hoped from finding you here that you had some motive beyond merely enjoying yourself, which is, after all, not the end of life.'

'I have come to that conclusion myself, Allerton, but, I am afraid, a little late.'

The unexpected mildness of the reply disarmed the lawyer ; there was also a tone of penitence in it still more surprising, and which, he rightly judged, could be only attributable to some new and gentle influence.

'With a man of your age, nothing in the way of amendment can be too late,' he answered. 'Notwithstanding all that has come and gone yet, there is nothing to despair of in your case. The race of life, to use a metaphor that is familiar to you, is in heats; we have most of us more than one run for our money; you have lost the first heat, that is all.'

'For my part,' returned the young lord grimly, 'I am inclined to think life a toss-up—the best out of three to win—and that I have lost the first toss. In either case the chances against me are considerable. Five to two is the betting, but the real odds are three to one.'

'As a very old friend, and one, I hope, incapable of an impertinence,' observed the lawyer gently, 'might I hazard a guess at the particular " event " you have on your mind, Cheribert?'

'There is no need to guess; you may take it, if you please, for granted,' replied the young man frankly.

'Let me say at once, then, that I am glad to hear you tell me so,' answered Mr. Allerton cordially. 'For a man in your position there is always a fresh start in life—unless, indeed, he makes a false one—in marriage. His past is forgotten; his future is once more in his own hands.'

'And the lady's,' suggested the young lord, smiling.

'Just so; and in the case we are considering it could not be better placed. It would be idle, however, to conceal from you, Cheribert, that there will be great difficulties in what you are proposing to yourself—difficulties in gaining your father's consent, difficulties as regards the law; though in both these matters you may rely on my doing my very best to help you.'

'You have again forgotten the lady,' observed the other dryly.

'No, I have not. There will also, as you say, be difficulties no doubt, in that quarter. It will be, of course, absolutely necessary that you should possess the same faith.'

'All right. I am completely at her disposal so far: a very easy convert.'

'Cheribert, I am astonished at you! On a subject of this kind I did hope you would forbear to jest.'

'Still, one of us, as it seems, will have to do it.'

It is quite right to be simple and un-sophisticated, but people ought to know where to stop, at all events to refrain from blurting out unpleasant truths. Mr. Allerton felt quite embarrassed.

'The case of Miss Grace,' he answered obliquely, 'is very peculiar. She is not devoted to the faith of her fathers.'

'As *I* am,' murmured the young lord, but the other ignored the sarcasm.

'In point of fact,' he continued with a forced smile, 'it is doubtful whether our old friend " Josh " was ever a Jew at all; it is my belief he only pretended to be so with the object of making himself unpleasant as a testator. His family were not brought up in that religion, or, if they were, only very loosely. I am pretty sure we shall not find that matter an insuperable obstacle.'

'I am quite sure of it,' observed Lord Cheribert dryly.

The reply, and still more the tone of it, was far from satisfactory to his companion, but it was a relief to him to have done with the topic.

'Well, what I venture to advise, Cheribert, is that there should be as little delay as possible in proceeding with this very important matter. Something has come to my knowledge — which you must excuse my going into—that makes it highly desirable that you and the young lady should come to some mutual understanding. It has nothing to do with the other matters which are pressing upon your attention, though I need hardly say that they would cease to be so very urgent in case the affair in question could be brought to a successful issue.'

'It seems to be rather a matter of business, nevertheless,' observed the young man coldly.

'My dear Cheribert, your position does not admit of your settling your matrimonial affairs with the same ease as yonder plough-boy, nor even as a young gentleman such as Mr. Walter Sinclair, for example, with no impediments of birth and rank, not to mention other encumbrances of your own making.'

The lawyer waited a moment to see whether the mention of Sinclair's name awakened any sign of suspicion in his young friend, but it seemed to have made no impression upon him whatever. His face was graver far than he had ever seen it, but quite unruffled. 'Yes, Cheribert,' he continued, ' for you—if you insist upon plainness of speech—marriage must be to some extent a bargain. There must be give and take on both sides; certain stipulations must be made; certain arrangements, tacit or expressed, agreed upon. It will not be necessary, of course, for you to go into them with the lady herself: her own good sense will point them out to her. She will understand that there are, and must be, contingencies—but you are not, I perceive, favouring me with your attention.'

The lawyer spoke with severity, and like a man whose feelings were hurt; his tone, rather than what he said, roused the other from his abstraction.

If Mr. Allerton imagined that mere weariness of serious talk—as, indeed, had often been the case before—was affecting his companion he did him an injustice. Lord Cheribert was serious enough himself, though it was quite true that he had not heard one word of what the other had just addressed to him.

'Pardon me, Allerton,' he said in his gentlest manner and with his most winning smile, 'I am not unconscious, believe me, of the good service you were trying to do me; I was only wondering how it came about that it should be worth your while, or any man's while, to take so much trouble on my account, being, as I am, such a worthless vagabond.'

'I should not permit your enemies—if, indeed, you have any—to say that in my hearing, my lord,' said the lawyer gently. He was touched by the young man's self-abasement; if only his father could see him at this moment, was his inward thought, how smooth things would be made for him!

'You would do all that is kind and friendly, I am quite sure,' continued Lord Cheribert gravely, 'but that would not alter the fact, you know, nor people's opinion of me.'

'Let us hope that *everybody* at all events will not be of that opinion,' said Mr. Allerton, smiling significantly. 'I would put that to the test at once if I were you.'

'But how should she *know*?' said the young man bitterly. 'It is a noble reflection, indeed, to feel that one's hope of happiness in the future lies in a woman's ignorance of one's past.'

'It is a position, nevertheless, in which a good many men who go a-wooing must needs find themselves,' returned the lawyer dryly; '"faint heart never won fair lady," my lord, is a good motto. I am bound for town to-day, as you know; will it be too much to ask of you to drop me a line to say how you have prospered in this matter?'

Lord Cheribert nodded and held out his hand, which the other warmly grasped. Two men with less in common as to pursuits and opinions it would have been difficult to find; the difference in their ages, great as it was, was slight compared with the diversity of their minds; but they had a very genuine friendship for one another; the lawyer had never felt his regard for his young client so strongly, which afterwards, through certain circumstances, became a source of satisfaction to him.

CHAPTER XXIV

AU REVOIR

As it is better, the doctors tell us, to leave off eating with an appetite than to stuff ourselves to repletion, so it is with respect to taking holiday. It is quite possible to have too much of even pleasure and leisure, as idle people find to their cost. To the toiler, bound to be back at his work by a certain date, it often seems the height of happiness if, like more fortunate men, he could reman *sine die* by the seaside, or at the lakes, where he has spent such happy days; he thinks that he could never tire out the welcome that kindly Nature for so brief a space has offered him. But in this he is mistaken. Amusement' without work, too far prolonged, is like veal without bacon, or sturgeon, a fish that is thought very highly of by those who have not tasted it. To Walter Sinclair, when the time came for him to return to town, it seemed that in leaving Elm Place he was quitting Eden. There was no such compulsion on him as there was with our first parents; but he had business in town in connection with that civil engineer affair about which he had unfortunately taken Mr. Allerton into his confidence; the lawyer had aided him in the matter, and an appointment had been made with certain persons which he could hardly decline to keep. Moreover, Mr. Allerton was bound for town himself, and had offered to be his travelling companion. There was only a week or two more in which river life could have had its attractions for him, but still he was loth to leave it; and much he envied Lord Cheribert, who, as he imagined (though on this particular occasion he was mistaken), was free to go or stay as he pleased, wherever

he would. He had had no previous acquaintance of the pleasures of home, and far less of
a home of pleasure, and he would have
thoroughly enjoyed himself but for a vague
longing for a certain something which he felt
to be beyond his reach. His general views of
life, which, if somewhat crude, were honest
and wholesome enough, had in no way
altered; rank was to him still but the guinea-
stamp, and personal merit the only test of
superiority that he acknowledged; but he
had become aware during the last few weeks
that other people, for whom he had a respect,
and who had treated him with hospitality,
thought very differently about these things.
The comforts and luxuries with which he had
seen them surrounded, though he cared little
or nothing for them himself, had made an
impression on him; he felt that to those who
were accustomed to them they might appear
as necessary as his short black pipe and screw
of tobacco were to him, and of course he had

not the power to bestow them. He knew nothing of the provisions of Mr. Tremenhere's will, but believed all of the ladies to be heiresses, and though he had been a gold-digger Walter Sinclair was not a fortune-hunter.

There was nothing in Indian life that had so disgusted him—for he had not had the same cruel experience of it that his father had had—as their treatment of their women, who toiled and slaved for them while they took their pleasure. To him a woman was not only an object of reverence but something to be worked for, and he would have scorned to owe his wealth to the bounty of a wife. Nevertheless, Grace Tremenhere was as sweet and attractive to him as the flower to the bee, though he had no intention of making honey out of her; and he found it a much sadder business than he expected, when the time came, to say 'good-bye' to her. Considering that she was only one of his three hostesses, and not the chief one, it might have been thought that he might have been contented with a general farewell; but somehow, though he would have shaken hands, even had it been for the last time, with the two elder sisters in the presence of each other without the least embarrassment, he felt that his *au revoir* to Grace (for he had been encouraged, we know, to come to Cumberland) should be said to her alone.

He found his opportunity on the camp shed, where from the other bank he had seen her walking alone before breakfast, and shot across in his skiff like an arrow from the bow, to join her.

'You are an earlier riser than your friends, Mr. Sinclair,' she observed with a welcoming smile.

'It has not been necessary for them as it has often been for me,' he said, 'to shoot or catch their breakfasts; and the habit lasts when the necessity no longer exists.'

'For my part,' she replied, 'I love the

early summer mornings, and am always out in them, though I have never felt the spur you speak of; if I had to catch my breakfast, to judge by my usual performance with the fishing-rod, I should be dreadfully hungry before I got it.'

'Heaven forbid, Miss Grace, that you should ever know such straits,' he answered fervently.

'Why not? On the contrary, I have come to the conclusion that it would be better for all of us—just as every German has to be a common soldier—if we had some personal experience of the hard lot that falls to so many of our fellow-creatures. There is nothing like a personal experience for be-getting sympathy.'

'No; a hard life would not suit you, or rather, I should say (for I am sure you would bear it bravely), would not be suitable to you. The spectacle of it,' he added gently, ' would, moreover, be distressing to others.'

' And who am I, and what have I done, Mr. Sinclair, that I should be exempt from the common lot of humanity ? ' she answered, smiling, but with some touch of indignation too. ' Do you picture me as designed by Providence to loll in a carriage and think of everybody on foot as beneath my notice ? '

' Oh no, oh no,' he answered softly; ' my view of you is very different. You remember our glorious day last week at Windsor, and how we enjoyed that noble park, which has not its rival, so far as I know, in all the world ? Well, to me, Miss Grace, you are very like that park.'

The colour rushed to her cheeks, though she made him a mock courtesy as if at the extravagance of the compliment.

' Oh, I don't mean that way only,' he said simply, ' but in your relation to others. Some of my friends, with whom on most other matters I agree, think that that park is too large a place to be used for what *they* call "ornamental purposes"—a poor phrase, in my opinion, to apply to its historic and native splendours; they want it to be turned into allotments for the benefit of the poor. That might do good to a few people of the present generation and rob all England that is to be of its brightest jewel. *You* would make an excellent allotment, no doubt—I mean, if you had to work for your bread, you would do it better than most young ladies; but it would be a waste of power, just as it would be in me, should I become the great engineer Mr. Allerton is so good as to prophesy, to knock nails in a boiler; while at the same time the effect which you and your surroundings produce upon all beholders would be lost.'

'It seems that my surroundings are of some importance,' she answered dryly.

'Not so important as appropriate,' he replied; 'the most beautiful picture owes something to its frame, and may even suffer from bad mounting; you would not have a jewel set in pewter.'

Though he spoke the language of flattery it was without its tone; his air, if an air of any kind could be imputed to him, was one of quiet conviction. Grace resented this exceedingly, though she did not recognise the reason; she had begun to have a greater liking for this jewel set in pewter, or let us say this 'rough diamond,' than she was herself aware of, and to be desirous of his good opinion, but by no means of this sort of homage.

A true woman prefers to be admired for something that belongs to herself, be it ever so small a thing, rather than for the advantages of her position—for her carriage (for instance) rather than for her carriage and horses. She dislikes to be placed on a pinnacle by one for whom she has a genuine regard, because it means isolation. Distance may lend enchantment to the view, but the remark is not flattering to the object.

'I am not accustomed to receive these high-flown compliments, Mr. Sinclair,' she said stiffly.

'If I have offended you let my ignorance plead for me,' he answered humbly. 'As to compliments, I was not aware that I was paying them; and as to high-flown ones, they would be altogether beyond my reach. I need not tell you that I am unaccustomed to the ways of you and yours: still, I should be sorry, very sorry, for you to think me that worst kind of boor who clothes his fustian thought in tinsel.'

'Indeed, indeed, I did not think so.'

'Thanks, Miss Grace. You would not hurt a fly, far less the feelings of a man who (I hope you know) is deeply grateful to you, and who would do all he could to show it.'

'I take your good will for granted,' she answered, smiling, 'but I am at a loss to know in what I have laid you under an obligation.'

'I suppose so,' he answered simply ; 'you are as ignorant—if I may once more recur to my unfortunate metaphor—as Windsor Park itself of the benefits you bestow. It is well, no doubt, that it should be so ; though, since you take such pleasure in the happiness of others, it seems a pity you should be unaware of conferring it. To me, Miss Grace, these last few weeks have been the happiest days I ever spent, or ever shall spend.'

He paused and looked at her with such tender earnestness and gratitude that her eyes drooped before his gaze. 'The river life is so pleasant,' she said hurriedly, 'and we have been so fortunate in the weather.

'Yes ; but it seems to me that there would be sunshine in Elm Place even though it were blowing blizzards. Well, that is over,' he added with a sigh, 'and I am come to say good-bye. I return this morning with Mr. Allerton to town.'

She was unaware that any such arrangement had been made, and the news affected her strongly; she felt her heart 'go' in a most unusual manner, and then, like a swimmer who has overspent himself, sink down, down; she knew that her voice trembled, in spite of all her efforts to keep it calm, as she replied:

'We shall all, I am sure, miss you very much, Mr. Sinclair.'

'That seems to be impossible, though it is pleasant hearing,' he answered gently. 'I am not much accustomed to be missed; and of all the homes in England I should think this one the most independent of a stranger's coming or going.'

How little, she thought, must this man know of her home! But his lack of perception of its true character was a recommendation to her rather than otherwise; it was no want of observation, as she well understood, for he was shrewd enough, that caused his ignorance, but the sense of gratitude for his hospitable reception which had blinded him. She was touched, too, by his humility in the matter, because it was not in accordance with his nature, of which she had made unconscious note.

'I am sorry that you should still consider yourself a stranger to us,' she answered kindly

'I am endeavouring not to consider myself at all,' he replied impulsively. The words were significant enough, but the tone in which they were uttered bespoke an intense emotion; directly they had left his lips he would have recalled them; the confession of his inmost thought had been rapture to him—a certain desperate wild delight—but he now bitterly accused himself for having expressed it. It was selfish, it was cowardly; it was not in his power, perhaps, to have given his companion pain, but it was evident that he had caused her embarrassment; a silence ensued between them which was more expressive than any commentary. Grace herself felt as if she could have bitten her tongue out for having given him what must have seemed 'an encouragement,' and was resolved, since he took such advantage of his opportunities, that he should not have another. 'I mean,' he stammered, 'that I shall always think of Elm Place as something apart from the rest of the world, myself included. There are some scenes, as I dare say you have felt, which strike one so by their restful beauty, that when we recall them they seem to have belonged to some other sphere, and to be apart from our personal experience.'

'Really? I have no recollection of any such, but then I have not enjoyed your advantages of travel.'

'My advantages!' he answered bitterly; 'the compulsory wanderings of a vagabond are not generally looked upon in that light. I do not flatter myself for a moment that I shall be remembered here. If one of your sisters should some day say to you, "Do you recollect that uncouth young fellow from

America or somewhere who used to visit us when we lived on the river?" and you are so good as to say "Yes," I know I ought to be perfectly satisfied; but on my side my feelings will be very different. I came here utterly unknown to you all, as indeed I still am; I am not such a fool as to suppose that, like Lord Cheribert, I bring my welcome with me, and yet I have been received with the same hospitality and kindness; it is an experience I am not likely to forget, believe me.'

Again his tone, freighted with tenderness and pathos, conveyed infinitely more than his words; his thanks, too, which by rights were due to Miss Agnes as head of the house, seemed to Grace, though he had not actually said so, to be addressed to her personally.

Under ordinary circumstances it would even so have been easy enough for her to acknowledge them; but she found it far from easy. She could not trust her voice to speak for her. Fortunately at that moment Rip came running down the lawn to them, and leapt into her arms.

'Here is one friend who at least should always remember you, Mr. Sinclair.'

'The dear little doggie! Well, even if he owed me something for pulling him out of the lasher, he has since repaid me fifty fold.'

The little creature, if he had but known it, was adding to his obligations now; its dumb caresses reminded the girl of the moment when she had seen this young fellow leap into the flood to save her favourite, like a river-god, but without the security of his immortality. How nearly he had perished for little Rip's sake—and hers! It was necessary that she should hide her heart indeed from him, since she felt utterly unable to harden it.

'Though I say good-bye, Miss Grace,' he continued after a pause, 'it is not, I am glad to think, for the last time.'

'Indeed?' she smiled and raised her eyebrows, as if in pleased surprise.

'Did you not know,' he stammered, 'that your sister had invited, at least had spoken of there being good fishing in the neighbourhood of your Cumberland home, and kindly expressed a wish that I should try it ?'

'To be sure,' she cried ; 'I had forgotten.'

His countenance fell, and he turned deadly pale.

It was cruel of her, but not so cruel to him as to herself; for while she thus kept him at arm's length, and further, she was hugging the dog to her bosom for his sake.

'It was only natural you should have done so,' he answered calmly; 'to you it must have seemed so very small a matter; but on my side—as I was just saying—things look so differently. Good-bye, Miss Grace.'

'But will you not breakfast with us ?'

'No, thanks, no. I will just go in and take leave of your sisters. Good-bye, little doggie'—he took up the little creature's paw —'I owe you many thanks. Your mistress will not even shake my hand, so I shake yours.'

Grace laughed and put out her hand, which trembled as he took it ; ' I do not say good-bye,' she said, ' because it is only, it seems, to be *au revoir.*'

It was not much to say, nor was the manner with which it was said, though gracious, particularly encouraging ; but to Walter Sinclair, though there was nothing of exultation in his manner of taking leave, for it was respectful even to reverence, it seemed a great deal, and made a great difference.

CHAPTER XXV

A DETERMINED SUITOR

BREAKFAST that morning at Elm Place was even a duller meal than usual. The two elder sisters never seemed to wake up to life till Mr. Roscoe and the rest crossed the river; they sat in sullen silence, save when it was absolutely necessary to speak to one another, and were so studiously and pointedly polite to Grace (to show how they could appreciate a kinswoman worthy of their attention) that she almost wished they had sent her also to Coventry. Nevertheless, she always did her best to keep up the conversation, though it was like playing lawn tennis alone against a double. But this morning, somehow, she was not equal to the strain. The words

Walter Sinclair had spoken to her with such passionate energy, 'I am endeavouring not to think of myself at all,' were still ringing in her ears; she had recognised their meaning, but not what had caused their utterance; if he had said, 'I am endeavouring not to think of *you*,' he could hardly have expressed himself more plainly. And why should he endeavour not to think of her? At the moment this question, which had naturally suggested itself, had filled her with vague suspicions of him. There had been that in his manner which she could not mistake for mere friendship—a tenderness, hidden by the veil of an exaggerated admiration, or forcibly repressed. The idea of the difference of their positions, as regarded wealth, never entered into her mind, and would have seemed to her, had it done so, to be the last to enter into his; she did not understand how independence of character could be associated with a humility born of convention—it was more

probable that there were other and far
stronger reasons for his reticence. As he
had said himself, he was a stranger to them
still ; concealment, indeed, of any kind,
seemed foreign to his character ; but, for
all she knew about him, he might have
been a married man ; the idea was abhorrent
to her, and had been dismissed at once, for,
in truth, she believed him incapable of a
baseness, but there was certainly *something*
that tied his tongue. Moreover, with the
inconsistency of her sex, she resented his
having spoken to her even as he had done,
upon so short an acquaintance, and on such
very slight encouragement. It had therefore
come to pass that she had ' snubbed ' him—or
(as it now appeared to her) had treated him
with unnecessary and uncalled-for harshness.
To pretend to have forgotten that he had
been invited to come to the North, had been
in particular, she felt, a piece of wanton
cruelty ; and his humble reply, ' It was only

natural you should have forgotten,' was as an arrow that had gone home to her very heart. She had, it was true, at parting, shown that she took it for granted they were to meet again, but she had not even expressed a wish that they should do so, as she would have done to any ordinary guest; and now, alas! she knew the reason why. He had not been an ordinary guest, but one that her heart had been entertaining in its inmost chamber, unawares, and she had only discovered it when it was too late. After such a dismissal, it was hardly likely that he would risk a second one, and it was probable that she had lost him for ever. It was no wonder that her heart was heavy within her and her tongue slow to speak. She found balm, however, in a Gilead where she least expected it, and where the soil did not often produce that commodity.

'So you had your " good-bye " from Mr. Sinclair on the camp-shed, I suppose, Grace?'

said Miss Agnes; 'I hope he was as effusive as he was to us.'

'He seemed very grateful for such hospitality as we were able to show him,' answered Grace gently.

'Grateful! I never had my hand so squeezed before!' continued Agnes; 'one would have thought I had given him a thousand pounds.'

Philippa broke into a little laugh, not, it is to be feared, at the pleasantry, which, indeed, was hardly deserving of it, so much as at the want of experience in hand-squeezing to which the speaker had so imprudently confessed.

'However, he is an honest young fellow,' continued Agnes, 'and I was glad to hear him renew his promise of looking in upon us at Halswater.'

For this good news, had it not been for the presence of her other sister, and from fear that the action might be imputed to an association of ideas, Grace could have thrown her arms round Agnes's neck and kissed her.

'We are going to lose Mr. Allerton this morning also,' observed Philippa, and in the afternoon Lord Cheribert. It is very inconsiderate of the gentlemen thus to desert us all together.'

'Is Lord Cheribert going?' inquired Grace with interest.

'Yes; did you not know it?'

The two elder ladies exchanged significant glances; the 'little affairs' of their younger sister were common ground, and almost the only ones on which they could meet without bickering.

'No, I did not know it,' said Grace. 'We shall miss him very much.'

'You did not favour Mr. Sinclair, my dear, with that expression of your regret,' observed Agnes slyly.

'We have known Lord Cheribert longer,'

replied Grace innocently, but blushing to her ear-tips.

' To be sure ; I suppose we have seen him twice before,' remarked Philippa with quiet enjoyment, ' which, of course, makes a great difference.'

Grace felt that her sisters were amusing themselves at her expense, but bore it with great sweetness, and the more easily since, with all their sagacity, it was clear that they were altogether on a false scent. It was not in human nature to resist leading them a little farther astray.

' I suppose Lord Cheribert is going simply because he is tired of us,' she observed with a little pout ; ' there can be no business to demand his attention.'

' Well, it isn't exactly business, of course, my dear,' said Agnes soothingly ; ' but you know how he is wedded—for the present— to sporting affairs ; it is to keep some appointment at a steeplechase, I believe, that he is obliged to be away. But it is to be his last appearance in the saddle; after which he will be reconciled to his father, and assume his proper position in the world.'

'When, I suppose, we shall never see him again,' observed Grace with a little sigh.

'That remains to be proved, my dear,' said Agnes encouragingly. 'Like Mr. Sinclair, he has *promised*, you know, to come and see us at Halswater. It would be only civil, by the bye, if you were to remind him of it; then, if he *does* come, we shall know the reason, shall we not?'

'We shall be able, at all events, to make a tolerable guess at it,' smiled her sister.

Like a general whose courage has carried him too far into the enemy's country, Grace would have been now very ready to retreat from the position whither her little joke had carried her, when, fortunately, she was released by the arrival of the subject of their conversation, in company with Mr. Roscoe, by boat. Mr. Allerton had sent his apologies for not taking leave in person; he had overslept himself, and had no time to spare to catch the train for town. The shadow of departure seemed to sit upon Lord Cheribert's face; he was so much more silent than usual that Agnes rallied him upon it.

'How could it be otherwise,' he said gently, 'since I too am leaving Elm Place? We are like boys whose holiday is over and are going back to work.'

'Yet somebody has just been saying that your life is all holiday,' observed Agnes, laughing.

'Indeed! I am afraid she meant, however, all idleness, which is something very different,' answered the young man gravely; he did not look towards Grace, but she knew that he attributed the remark to herself, and would have given much to have been able to disclaim it. She would have, somehow, preferred that he should not take notice of her at all that morning.

This, however, was not to be. Agnes soon left the room, on pretence of some matters of the house requiring her attention, and Philippa took Mr. Roscoe out with her upon the lawn, perhaps without design (for she never lost an opportunity of being alone with him), but after what her sisters had been saying to Grace, it had an uncomfortable sense to her of design. Lord Cheribert and herself were thus left alone.

'As it is my last morning, Miss Grace,' he said with his pleasant smile, but in a tone much more serious than usual, ' might I ask a favour of you?' Before she could reply (a circumstance for which she felt strangely thankful) he added, ' It is only that we should take that walk on the hill together which we took when I first came.'

She answered, as lightly as she could, ' By all means,' and put on her hat, which ' on the

river' ladies have never to go far for. As
they left the house she stopped to call the
dog—a natural action enough, but one which
she had never before felt so impelled to do;
it was extraordinary how much dearer
Rip had grown to be to her within the last
hour.

'How fond you are of that little creature!
it ought to be a happy doggie,' said Lord
Cheribert.

'I don't know about that; but he likes, I
think, to be with me—" the off-and-on companion of my walks," as Wordsworth calls it.'

'I wish I was good at poetry,' sighed the
young man; 'but, unfortunately, I am good
at nothing.'

'I should be sorry to think that, Lord
Cheribert.'

'But you *do* think it; how can it be otherwise? Not that I mind your doing it—that
is, of course, I wish I were more worthy of
your good opinion; but I had rather be

brought to book by you—by Jove, I would—
than praised by other people!'

'I was really not aware that I had ever
" brought you to book," as you call it, Lord
Cheribert.   I suppose it's a sporting expression.'

'Don't laugh at me, please, Miss Grace,'
he answered humbly; 'scold me as much as
you please—it does me good; but don't laugh
at me.'

'It is rather difficult to help it, when you
talk of my doing you good.'

'Ah, but you do.   No one in the world
has ever done it but you.   Schoolmasters have
tried it, dons have tried it, the governor has
tried it; but they might just as well have
thrown water on a duck's back.   I was dry
the next moment.   But from the day I first
saw you—no, the day you had the kindness
to talk to me in this very place—Heaven knows
how long ago, but it seems a century——'

'That is not very complimentary to your

entertainers at Elm Place,' she put in quietly.

'Now, you are laughing again at me; I don't think you would do it if you knew how cruel it was. What I mean is, not that the time has been heavy on my hands here, Heaven knows, but that what has happened to me seems more important than all that has happened anywhere else. I feel as if half my life has been passed here and half elsewhere; and the two halves have been *so* different!'

He paused and she said ' Yes ?'—a ridiculous and ineffectual monosyllable, as she was well aware; but what *was* she to say? His manner was so earnest, his tone so tender, his look so beseeching, that she could hardly believe it was Lord Cheribert.

'There is a verse, I know not from what author, the governor used to be fond of quoting to me on a Sunday,' he continued, "Between the stirrup and the ground, mercy I sought, mercy I found "—a religious version, I suppose, of " It's never too late to mend," and one, I conclude, which he thought especially applicable to me as a racing man. If Providence is really so kind to a sinner, cannot you also hold out some hope to him ? '

They were standing on a spur of the hill, with the wood at their back and a great expanse of landscape beneath them ; the river with its fairy fleet winding for miles till it shrank to a thread ; men and women at their labour in the fields ; cattle in their pasture ; but not a sound came up to them. The world seemed to be lying at their feet, but they two far removed from it. It was a scene one of them never forgot.

' It is not to an ignorant girl like me that you should apply, Lord Cheribert, in such matters as you speak of ; they are altogether too high for me. I can only say with one of the greatest of our fellow-creatures on his deathbed, " Be a good man ; nothing else can comfort you." '

' That is all that I want you to say, Grace, provided only that you will teach me to be one. Priests are no use to me. It is from you alone that I have learnt to understand my own worthlessness. My fate is in your hands.'

' In *mine*, my lord?' she answered with a faint pretence of misunderstanding him. ' What would you have me do?'

' Give me your love; or, if that is impossible, as indeed it well may be at present, give me hope. I can be patient enough with such a prize in view, and though I shall never be worthy of it, I will try, every day and every hour, to make myself more so. You see, dear Grace'—here he smiled so brightly that it seemed hard indeed to say him nay—'I have so many advantages on my side; every step which is not astray, and of which other men would have nothing to congratulate themselves upon, will be to me a clear gain; I have been, until I knew you, so exceedingly disreputable. You may say, indeed,' he continued cheerfully, 'that that of itself is no recommendation ; but when you see me or hear of me becoming more and more as you would wish me to be, and know that it is all your doing, you will begin to take just a little pride in me, as in the work of your own hands. When people ask me, as they will be sure to do, what is the meaning of this reformation, I shall tell them—but gently and not passionately—to mind their own business, until I have your permission to explain matters ; for a day will come—I feel sure of it—when you will not be ashamed of acknowledging me as your disciple ; a day when my father will ask me in his solemn way, " What has snatched you like a brand from the burning ? " and I shall reply to him in his own language, " Grace." '

' Lord Cheribert,' replied the girl with dignity, ' if it were anyone but yourself who is thus speaking to me, I should say that it was impossible that what you express so lightly could be seriously intended.'

'It's my unfortunate way of speaking,' interposed the young man humbly. 'I am—that is, I used to be—frivolity itself, I know; but it's only manner.'

'I am aware of it. I also feel that it would be quite inconsistent with your nature to give anyone, designedly, a moment's pain. It would give *me* pain—very great distress of mind, Lord Cheribert—to discuss the matter which you have so unexpectedly forced upon my attention.'

'Forced! Good Heavens!' A look of unutterable sorrow crossed the young man's face.

'Forgive me; I was unnecessarily harsh. I wanted to stop you. The thought of your father—since you have mentioned him—ought, in my opinion, to have kept you silent. I know little of the world's ways; but setting all other objections, even more important, though not less grave, aside, can it be imagined for a moment that your father would approve of what you have just been saying?'

'My father!' he exclaimed contemptuously; 'What can he give me in place of you that I should consult his wishes? What has he ever done for me that can be matched with what *you* have done? What is he in my eyes as compared with you? Nothing, and less than nothing.'

'You ought to be ashamed to say so, Lord Cheribert,' she answered indignantly. '*My* father is dead, yet his memory is a more sacred thing than any living man can give me. You talk of reformation, but it seems to me that reformation, like charity, should begin at home.'

'You are right, Grace; you are always right,' returned the young man with an air of quiet conviction. 'I will be dutiful to him, because you tell me it is my duty, and therefore it must be so. His consent shall be obtained, at whatever price. My pride shall bend its neck, and he shall put his foot upon it.'

'But that is only one thing, Lord Cheribert, and not the greatest thing, that puts a barrier between you and me.'

She spoke with firmness, even with vigour; but at the same time she recognised her mistake in having permitted herself, even for a moment, to be drawn into a discussion of details. The determination in his face, which had suddenly become cold and calm, as though it had been hewn in marble, appalled her.

'That I can easily believe, dear Grace,' he answered gently. 'No one can expect to get to heaven express and without stoppages. If you will be kind enough to mention your objections, I will tick them off on my fingers —or, if you will permit me, what will be far better, on yours—and answer them, one after another, as well as I can.'

It was very difficult to deal with such a lover; passionate as Rousseau, resolute as Wellington, but in manner a *farceur*. It was as natural to Lord Cheribert to be droll in the most serious situations as for a dull man to be serious in a droll one. Like a planet (which was also, alas! a falling star), he dwelt in an atmosphere of his own, which, while by no means one of mere persiflage, was of exceeding levity.

'I will mention one obstacle to your suit, since you compel me to do so,' answered Grace gravely, 'which, I am sure you will agree with me, can leave no more to be said. I am deeply touched by the honour you have done me, and I shall never cease to be your friend and well-wisher; but I do not love you, Lord Cheribert.'

He bit his lip and turned a little pale, then smiled again as pleasantly as ever.

'It would be quite beyond my utmost expectations if you did, dear Grace,' he answered gently; 'but I have—as regards yourself at least—a plentiful stock of patience, and an immense reserve of what our friends call obstinacy and ourselves resolution.

You shall teach me everything else, and I will teach you to love me.'

'It is impossible, my lord; I shall never learn that lesson.'

He looked at her for a moment in silence; the dog came barking from the wood, and ran to its mistress, who took it up in her arms. For the first time Lord Cheribert's pleasant face was clouded with a frown.

'Perhaps,' he said, 'you have learnt it already from some other teacher? That is a question which, if you could read my heart, you would not refuse to answer; my *life* hangs on it.'

She buried her face in that of her little favourite to hide the flush that overspread her cheeks.

'I must have your " yes " or " no," Grace,' he continued with tender earnestness. ' Are you engaged to another man ? '

She looked up at him haughtily, almost defiantly.

'No, I am not, my lord; but that can make no difference.'

The young man uttered a sigh of relief: then broke into a laugh full of joyful music. 'Oh, but indeed it does,' he said; 'if you did but know how happy that reply has made me, you would never have the heart to take such happiness away. Do not spoil it by another word. I ask for nothing more—just now. You see how easily I am satisfied—which is a great recommendation in a husband.'

'My lord——'

'There now, I have angered you. Forgive me. Rip, you rascal, of whom I feel so jealous, ask your dear mistress to forgive me. It is the very last peccadillo of a lifetime. Let us change the subject and talk of something else. Which do you like best, Miss Grace, the river or the mountain, Elm Place or the Fells? Your sisters—and here they come with Roscoe the Inseparable—have recommended me to try the fishing in Halswater. I shall shortly, therefore, have the pleasure of meeting you again.'

'Believe me, Lord Cheribert, it will be useless,' she answered hastily, for the others were approaching them.

'I shall come if I am alive,' he answered quietly. 'Miss Tremenhere, what a view you have here ! I cannot believe, for all you tell me, that your Cumberland home can show a finer.'

'I hope you will come, then, and judge for yourself, as you have half promised to do, Lord Cheribert,' said Agnes graciously.

'Half promised ? Indeed I have whole promised,' returned the young man cheerfully. 'There is nothing which I look forward to with greater pleasure. I know when I am well off (it's a long time since I *have* been well off, as Mr. Roscoe knows), and if I have the same good time at Halswater as I have had at Elm Place, I shall have reason, indeed, to congratulate myself.'

CHAPTER XXVI

IN LAKELAND

THERE are two valleys in Lakeland, side by side, far removed from those which are familiar to its tourists, both of them beautiful, but with a beauty that owes little to verdure and less to foliage, each traversed by a rocky stream—in the one case by the Werdle, in the other by the Start—from which they take their names. In the Werdle valley there is a farm or two, a roadside inn, and a vicarage with a church in proportion to the value of the benefice, which it would be mockery indeed to call 'a living;' in the Start valley there are, where it is widest, but a few cottages, and where it narrows and the huge fells begin to hem it in, there is no sign of human habitation; there are no cattle, nor sheep. The hill fox and the foul-mart are to be found there, indeed, but only by those who know where to look for them; the very birds that haunt those solitary walls of rock are few; the rock raven and the buzzard hover over them. Past Werdle, and over the hill that separates it from its neighbour-valley, and up the Start vale at its head, is the mountain, road to Halswater. Many fair scenes and many fine ones are to be beheld by the pedestrian upon his way; but what will strike him most, not from its beauty, though it is very beautiful, but from the unexpected-ness of finding it amongst such wild and grim surroundings, is the view of a country-house. Until eight hundred feet or so of the pass has been ascended, Nature in her wildest garb alone presents herself to him; but presently, through a cleft in a much loftier mountain range, his eye falls on a glint of blue, which is the foot of Halswater; and on its sterile verge, as if dropped there from the clouds, a mansion with lawns and gardens belted with noble trees, like an oasis in the desert. To find such an abode of luxury and ease cradled in crag and fell is startling, but there is nothing in its appearance that jars upon Nature's grandeur; time has so mellowed what art so well began that it seems no more out of place than any other of those ancestral English homes which seem part and parcel of the landscape they adorn. The wonder of the beholder is how it got there. To have dragged the materials for building it over the way he has come would have defied even Egyptian labour. Five hundred feet higher, and the secret is disclosed to him; yonder lies the ocean; and even where he stands the discordant shriek of the hawk will, in wild weather, not seldom mingle with the whine of the sea-gull. It was said in old times that only two dalesmen knew the road to Halswater Hall, but the sailor always knew it. It was he who brought the oak for its panelling, the marble for its mantels, and the pictures for its gallery.

With the sea half-a-dozen miles or so away for its background, the mansion looks even a more enviable dwelling-place than at the first glance. But, like more humble homes, it has not been able to close its doors against misfortunes; not only have Disease and Death visited it in their never-omitted rounds, but even War has found its way there. In Cromwell's time, indeed, its position was so remote that it is written its inmates and their neighbours knew not of the existence of the Great Protector till he and his work had passed away, but in the later Stuart days Faction, jealous of its peaceful solitude, and disguised in the garb of Loyalty, made it a nest of treason. Then the sea brought ships by night, and the ships brought men, and the standard of Rebellion was raised where yonder clump of pines casts its shadows on the lake, and the mountain echoes learnt for the first time the sound of the trumpet. Then Authority came and with relentless foot crushed Rebellion out, and set her torch to the fair dwelling—where the mark of it can still be seen—and wrote her name in blood in all the peaceful valleys so deeply that it took generations to efface it. But one thing it left alive, veiled Discontent: and though there was no more war there was treason still, and the sea brought plotters from the north who lay *perdu* in the stately place, and priests who dwelt, like conies, in holes and corners of it, and once a fugitive, it is said, with a dark face but jovial mien, before whom Sir Eustace himself stood unbonneted, and who drank out of the only cup of silver the soldiers of the Hanoverian had left in the plate room.

Then the ancient family in time died out,

and though it could not be quite said that its memory had faded 'from all the circle of the hills,' its legends were giving place to gossip about the new-comers. A dozen years ago or so, one Mr. Joseph Tremenhere, from London, an individual supposed to be connected with commercial pursuits, had bought the place and renewed its glories, but in the modern fashion. The domestics were almost as many as of yore, and far more gorgeously attired; new pleasure-boats and a steam yacht were added to the house flotilla; the billiard-room was fitted up with gas-reflectors (a circumstance that set the very dale aflame); and it was even believed by some that ice was to be found on the dinner-table in the hottest summer day. Stories in this style of Eastern exaggeration were told of the hall and its owner by the landlord of the 'Fisher's Welcome' at the head of the lake, to amuse his guests when the wet weather, as it was wont to do in those parts, set in. Mr. Tremenhere had been a 'good sort,' it seemed, and thought no more of giving a guinea to a guide or a boatman than if it were a shilling; but he did not go to kirk, nor had he the excuse of belonging to the ancient faith as his predecessors at the Hall had done; for their chapel was now only used as a music gallery. It was hazarded by some gentleman sportsman at the 'Welcome' that Mr. Tremenhere might be a Jew—a pleasantry received with rapture, and one which in the neighbourhood (where jokes were scarce) was often quoted to the general enjoyment.

As to the members of his family, Miss Tremenhere was thought to be rather calm and stately, which in the mistress of so great a household seemed pardonable enough; Miss Philippa to be good-natured and very civil; but Miss Grace, all were agreed, was the flower of the flock. She had a good word for everyone, and an open hand (with something in it) wherever it was needed. There was much less mystery about the new proprietor of the Hall than there had been about the old ones, but Mr. Edward Roscoe puzzled folks. He always accompanied his patron on his summer holiday, but without sharing his diversions: for fishing he had apparently as little taste as skill; there were a few grouse on the hills about the house, but they suffered no diminution in their numbers at his hands; he did not seem to be moved by that passion for the picturesque which brought some harmless lunatics to Halswater; no one, in short, could understand why Mr. Roscoe was a standing dish at his host's table. At first they took him for the bridegroom elect of one of the two elder Miss Tremenheres, but in course of years that illusion vanished. They then concluded he was Mr. Tremenhere's secretary, as indeed he was, and something more. If they could have guessed the real nature of his duties, it would have astonished them exceedingly; for the owner of Halswater Hall had nothing in common with Josh of Lebanon Lodge, Kensington. He caught fish on his hook instead of men—the speckled trout and the scarlet char, in place of the nobility and the military—and placed them in stew-ponds to be devoured at leisure. He put the screw on none of his tenants, and therefore had no necessity of employing Mr. Roscoe's skill with that instrument; and yet that gentleman was somehow as unpopular as an Irish landlord's agent under the Plan of Campaign. When the news came to his Northern home of Mr. Tremenhere's decease, the honest dalesmen were moved to sorrow, but found some mitigation of it in the reflection that now that they had lost the substance they would also lose the shadow that had dogged it; but in this they were fated to be mistaken.

When the three bereaved sisters arrived at the Hall, Mr. Roscoe arrived with them; only, instead of living under the same roof as of old, he was accommodated in a cottage in the grounds, which had been used by the old family, in the days of their hospitality, for overflow guests.

Matters were not so pleasant in the household as they had been at Elm Place. The presence of visitors had there had a restraining influence upon the two elder sisters, who, now that they were alone together, often said sharp things (in the sense of antagonism rather than cleverness, as Ajax was called *acerrimus* Ajax) to each other, and still sharper, in confidence, to Mr. Roscoe, *of* each other. That gentleman's position, though as general manager of so vast an establishment, and one in whom the most implicit trust was placed, it seemed to be enviable, had some crumpled rose-leaves about it, and even occasionally thorns. Each sister wanted the attention he paid to the other; but Agnes— which was curious, since she had usually more self-command—by far the more openly.

She 'could not understand why he gave himself the trouble to make such a fool of Philippa,' which was her way of stating that he spoilt her; to which he would reply with his most winning smile, 'It is for your sake,' which always pacified her.

It must not be imagined, however, notwithstanding this tenderness of speech, that anything he said to her could be construed into a declaration of love; nor did Agnes complain of this reticence—not so much, perhaps, because she was old enough to know better, as of a certain understanding which existed between them. With Philippa he was tender too, but in a less confidential way; and yet her too he contrived to keep in good temper. Mr. Edward Roscoe, indeed, deserved the name of a good manager even more than those who grudgingly enough bestowed it on him imagined; but no one knew what his success cost him. Moreover, with every day his position became more precarious, as is apt to be the case with those who have given 'promises to pay' without the possession of assets. It is true that there was no date on the bill, but it had to be renewed nevertheless, and the operation, though it had some likeness to a lover's quarrel, was by no means the renewal of love. He was pressed, too, from without (though that need not be referred to at present) as well as from within, and was already in such straits as might have made some men desperate. But though Edward Roscoe had nothing of what we call faith, he believed in Edward Roscoe, and, like all men of his type, was confident that time and chance would somehow work together in favour of so deserving an object.

Much more apart from him than her sisters, but hardly more ignorant of the plans he was devising, and in which she too had her place, stood Grace Tremenhere. Indeed she stood apart from her sisters also, though they still united in treating her, after their fashion, with tenderness. Of her at least they had no jealousy, and though to some degree she stood in their way, they did not visit that involuntary crime with their displeasure. In some respects, though their hopes rested on her having reached a marriageable age, they still considered her as a child; her presence softened their characters—long warped from what they might have been, and stunted by rivalry and discontent—and evoked what little remained to them of fun and freshness. Unfortunately for her peace of mind, their humour—as always happens with women of coarse natures—took the form of raillery about her supposed admirers. When the post came (at an hour when it leaves places less out of the world), they would pretend to look at the superscription of her letters, and were perpetually asking her when Lord Cheribert was to make his appearance. 'We told you, you know, that if he came we should know for certain what he came for, and his last words, as you remember, were that he intended to come.'

It was a very unwelcome as well as threadbare jest, but it was difficult for her to put a stop to it, and it was at least some comfort that their assurance of his lordship's intention prevented them from harping upon a still more tender string. If they had ever entertained a suspicion about Walter Sinclair, it was clear they had dismissed it. But as regarded the girl herself, it was certain that she thought of that young gentleman a good deal more than when he had been their visitor. He was not, of course, her lover; unlike Lord Cheribert, he had never breathed a word of love to her; but what he had said—his few vague phrases of repressed admiration—were recalled to her mind much oftener than the other's passionate and determined words. The remembrance of the latter filled her with alarm, and even with repugnance. She feared his perseverance and importunity, which in that lonely spot, surrounded by those who, far from having sympathy with her resistance, would be ranged upon the other side, would, she felt, be well-nigh intolerable. If she had but had Mr. Allerton to appeal to—for she had no idea that his influence had been thrown into the other scale—it would have been some comfort ; but she was absolutely without adviser, save the secret whispers of her high-beating heart.

If Walter—that is Mr. Walter Sinclair—should keep his promise of coming up to Halswater—but his doing so was doubtful ; fool that she was to have discouraged him !—then indeed—but even *that* was set with difficulties and embarrassments. Perhaps they might quarrel, and she be the unwilling cause ; these two young men, one of whom she liked so much—at a distance—and the other whom she—she did not say she loved even to herself, but a blush, though none was there to see it, spoke for her.

One night, as the ladies were thinking of retiring, a sound of wheels upon the broad gravel sweep made itself heard in the drawing-room; for by coming a score of miles and more from the nearest station the house was now approachable by wheels, which in the old time it had not been; then there was a peal at the front-door bell.

'He has come at last!' cried the elder sisters in a breath, and both of them looked significantly at Grace.

'The idea of his coming here instead of to the inn!' exclaimed Agnes; 'this is making himself at home indeed. You must put him up in the cottage, Mr. Roscoe.'

'You need not disturb yourself, Miss Agnes, nor need Miss Grace put on that heightened colour,' observed the gentleman appealed to. 'I hear a voice which is certainly not that of Lord Cheribert.'

'But who on earth can it be?' asked Agnes.

' Why, of course it's Mr. Roscoe's brother,' observed Philippa.

' How do you know that?' inquired Agnes, with sudden vehemence.

' I don't know it, I only guess it,' answered Philippa with an uneasy look, ' because, as you know, he has been expected for so long.'

Then the door opened and the butler announced Mr. Richard Roscoe.

CHAPTER XXVII

MR. RICHARD

THE man who was thus ushered for the first time into the presence of the Tremenhere family would have been remarkable anywhere, but in that splendid drawing-room, surrounded by all the accessories of wealth and luxury, his appearance was especially striking from its incongruity. He was dressed in what is known in the neighbourhood of Ratcliff Highway as ' slops,' a suit of ready-made clothes that hung on his gaunt, spare limbs like the attire of a scarecrow. It was, or had been, a sailor's suit, but he had not the least resemblance to a sailor. He had long brown hair, and a beard so deeply tinged with grey that it did not seem to match it. Though at

least six feet in height, he had not a superfluous ounce of flesh about him ; he was
emaciated and hollow-eyed, like one who
had endured great hardships ; to his brother,
who had a robust frame, and was attired in
faultless evening dress, he presented the
strongest contrast. They had absolutely
nothing in common. There was something
in the new-comer, however, which spoke of
vanished strength, or at least of great powers
of endurance : what could be seen of his
muscles stood out like whipcord. His eyes
were very expressive, wild as those of a hawk ;
perhaps at one time they might have been as
fierce, but they had now a hunted look in
them. A judge of physiognomy would have
pronounced this man to have passed through
some terrible experience.

The meeting between the brothers was
friendly, but not cordial. The new-comer
seemed to have some doubt of his welcome ;
while the other, despite his habitual self-

command, was evidently embarrassed. His manner was nervous, and he spoke with a rapidity that was quite unusual to him.

'So, Richard, you are come at last,' he said, as they shook hands. 'I am glad to see you, and I think I may say as much for my kind friends here.' And with that he introduced him to the sisters.

The visitor was evidently quite unaccustomed to society. As he took each lady by the hand he stared at her with unconcealed curiosity, and detained it in his grasp much longer than is common on a first acquaintance ; upon Grace he stared with an undisguised but by no means rude admiration ; it was like the natural admiration exhibited by the savage.

'You must excuse,' he said with an awkward smile, and in a hoarse voice, that spoke even more of ill-health than his wasted frame and the glitter of his eyes, 'what you find amiss in my manners ; I have not seen a lady for these ten years !'

'My brother Richard has been a back-woodsman,' explained Mr. Roscoe curtly.

'Well, scarcely that, Edward,' he replied dryly; 'you are doubtless thinking of the wild man of the woods; I have been a hunter on the prairie.'

Agnes exclaimed, 'How interesting!' Philippa laughingly observed, 'Like Leather-stocking.' Grace regarded him in thoughtful silence; she remembered that Walter Sinclair had described his father as having followed that calling, and expressed his own admiration for it.

'There is not much to hunt here, Mr. Richard, I fear,' continued Agnes, 'except the hill fox; but you are doubtless a fisherman, and we can promise you some sport in that way; and I dare say Grace, who is our mountaineer, will act as your guide over the hills. Anything we can do for Mr. Roscoe's brother will give us pleasure.'

The new-comer looked up with gratified surprise.

'I wish your sister a better office, Miss Tremenhere, but I thank you kindly.'

There was nothing of cringing or humility in his tone; but it was unmistakably one of astonishment at the nature of his welcome, as also of the surroundings. He seemed amazed at finding his own reflection in the mirrors (of which there were many in the drawing-room, for poor 'Josh's' taste in ornamentation had been French and florid), and now and then cast furtive glances at the gilded ceiling as though wondering how the gold had been made to stick to it.

'How long have you been in England, Mr. Richard?' inquired Agnes presently.

'In London only forty-eight hours; I came straight up from Liverpool, and only remained in town just to buy these things,' and he looked down at his slop suit with a painful sense of their inadequacy to the occasion.

'It was very good of you,' continued Agnes graciously, 'to leave all the attractions of town to come down to us at once.'

The new-comer looked embarrassed, and turned an inquiring glance towards his elder brother.

'I ventured to tell him that he would be welcome here,' explained Mr. Roscoe; 'and he was naturally, I hope, desirous to see me after the lapse of so many years.'

'It could hardly be otherwise,' observed Philippa.

'We are most pleased, I'm sure,' chimed in Agnes. And Grace too smiled acquiescence.

All which was a proof indeed of Mr. Roscoe's influence with the family, for it is one thing to welcome one's friend, and quite another to welcome one's friend's friend.

With all the good-will in the world, however, to put their guest at his ease the sisters found it a little difficult. There were, of course, excuses for him; he had not been used, as he himself had owned, to society; he knew nothing of his entertainers; after so long a separation even his brother could have hardly seemed familiar to him; but all these pleas having been allowed, it was still felt by the two elder ladies that Mr. Richard Roscoe was a little awkward: perhaps he suffered by comparison with that complete self-possession and ease of manner which they could never sufficiently admire in his elder brother; Grace thought him only shy. She pitied him, because she understood that he was poor, and had suffered privations. Her interest was always attracted by such persons, just as natures of another kind are attracted by those who are rich and prosperous. Yet even she too experienced a certain sense of relief when Mr. Roscoe took his brother away to the supper that had been prepared for him in the lodgings where he was to be bestowed.

The night was moonless and very dark. It would have been no easy matter even for one well acquainted with the grounds about the house to find his way to the cottage without damage to the flower-beds, if not to himself; but what seemed much more beautiful and striking to the stranger than any wonders of mere and fell that had met his eye that day, the whole garden was lit by gas-lamps. This too was owed to the taste of the departed Josh. The gas, of course, was made at home, or rather in a little wood apart from the house, which hid what was unsightly in the means of its manufacture; but the lamp-posts, very nicely gilded, had been imported from London. It was no wonder that Mr. Richard Roscoe opened his mouth as well as his eyes in astonishment at these artificial splendours.

' Well, I *am* darned ! this beats all ! '
he murmured, with hushed amaze.

At which involuntary tribute of admiration
Mr. Edward burst out laughing. It was not a
pleasant laugh, which was not his fault, for
he had scarcely any experience in laughing,
but it was a genuine one. The astonishment
of his relative at finding him in such very
luxuriant clover tickled him, because it was
a compliment to the intelligence which had
placed him there ; it was only himself who
knew that his position was not quite so
enviable as it appeared to be, and it gratified
him to see it thus so fully recognised by
one incapable of pretence or any stroke of
diplomacy. It even pleased him to see the
wonder with which this simple hunter of
the prairies regarded the glass and silver
upon the table laid for his entertainment,
and the obsequiousness of the servant in
attendance.

' If I had known of your arrival I would

have got you something better for supper,' observed Mr. Edward slily.

'Better! Why, I have not sat down to such a meal these five years.'

The answer was a little beyond the other's expectation. 'You need not wait, Thomas,' he observed curtly; 'I will look after Mr. Richard myself.'

It struck him a moment too late that it had been rather indiscreet in him to let the footman know that any brother of his had not been used to luxury from his cradle. He did not shut his eyes to the probability of the members of the Tremenhere household regarding him from quite another point of view than that of their mistress or mistresses; and though he was not one to care much for the opinion of the servants' hall, he felt it was foolish to have given them a handle for gossip. Slight as had been the incident, it sufficed to put a stop to the late feelings of self-glorification in which he had permitted himself to indulge, and to replace him in his usual attitude of cold serenity.

'You have not brought much luggage with you, Dick, I noticed,' he observed, lighting a cigar, while the other attacked the viands.

'And yet it looks more than it is,' replied the other frankly. 'I did not dare bring down the things I came over in; so the portmanteau is half empty.'

'The portmanteau! If you had only given me time, I would have seen that you had five portmanteaus.'

'Then you would have had to send me the money to buy them. I am stone broke.'

'I suppose so. Look here, Dick: you must never be without money in your pocket.' He now unlocked a drawer, and, taking out a handful of sovereigns, placed them beside his brother's plate.

The other coloured to his forehead. 'I was only joking,' he said, with an air of annoyance, and even of distress. 'I am not a schoolboy, that I should take a "tip" like that.'

'Take it as a loan then. You will very likely have no need to spend it; but it will not do for you—or, if you prefer that way of putting it, for *me*—to be without ready money. Ten pounds, man—what do you suppose is ten pounds, or a hundred, or a thousand, for that matter, to a man in my position?—and I don't choose my brother to be penniless.'

'That circumstance did not seem to distress you very much at one time,' returned the other dryly.

The reply was unexpected, and for a moment Mr. Edward's face looked very unlike that of a host—even a host at somebody else's expense; but the frown cleared away as quickly as it came.

'That's quite true,' he answered, laughing; 'but circumstances alter cases. If there was ever a time when we were like two beggars fighting for a crust, forget it. I have now, at all events, not only the will but the power to make you ample amends '

'I do not wish to live upon your bounty, Edward,' was the cold rejoinder; the speaker's eyes were still looking at the little heap of gold with marked disfavour.

'I wish I had given him a hundred,' was the other's reflection; 'it is merely avarice that takes this mask of pride.'

'You gave me to understand that if I came over here I should find employment of some kind.'

'So you shall, Dick. Do not fear that you will not be worth your wages.' Then added to himself, 'I do believe he is the same tom-fool he ever was; and I'm another to have ever sent for him on the belief that he could have altered.'

'But I should like to know what the employment *is*,' persisted Richard. He had not the resolution of his brother, the dogged determination that can tire out all ordinary opposition, and almost reverse the adverse decrees of fate; but he was not without a strain of it, as the other knew. 'When you wrote to me upon the matter, you spoke of it as being something well worth my while—or, as you expressed it, "any man's while"—but you did not even hint at what it was.'

'That is quite true, Dick; it was something that I could not set down in black and white.'

'Then I won't do it. I have been in trouble once—thanks to you—and that is enough,' was the vehement rejoinder. 'It shall never happen again—of that you may take your oath, Edward; or, rather, I will take *my* oath, which is much surer.'

'I forgive you your unbrotherly sentiments,' answered the other, in tones the quiet calmness of which contrasted strangely with the other's passion; 'the more so since I admit that there is some cause for them; but what I cannot understand is how a person of your intelligence can suppose me capable of making any proposition such as you hint at. You may say, of course, "But you *have* done things of that kind," to which I reply it is true that an individual of my name once did them—a wretched penniless adventurer—but he has nothing whatever in common with the person who is now addressing you. You have seen with your own eyes what I am here— the confidence in which I am held by your hostesses, who are the mistresses of millions. Can you think me such a fool as to risk it by doing anything discreditable?'

'I am speaking of what you may want *me* to do,' answered the other, to whom wine and good cheer seemed to have given both strength and spirit. 'You have confessed just now that you could not set it down in black and white.'

'How could I? It was a very delicate business, though one that was entirely free from illegality of any kind. Unhappily, your long delay has, I fear, caused the part I intended for you to be filled up by another. I can now promise you nothing so splendid; but there is much work to be done, of part of which you can relieve me, in connection with the Tremenhere estate, which, for the present at all events, will give you profitable occupation.'

'Out-of-door work, of course, I could do—overlooking and so forth—and I know something of grass-farming.'

'Your talents will, I am sure, be most useful,' said the other dryly.

'Mr. Tremenhere, I suppose, made you his executor?' observed Richard after a pause.

'Not a bit of it,' answered the other, with a contemptuous smile. 'I have made myself what you see I am; and you have not seen me at my best even yet,' he added, with a sudden burst of pride.

'What! Thane of Cawdor that shall be

King of Scotland! You mean to marry one
of them, do you?'

'There are things more unlikely to happen
in the world than that, Dick. To tell you
the honest truth, I was at one time in hopes
that you might have married the other.'

'The other? You mean Miss Philippa, I
suppose, since I can hardly flatter myself I
could have captivated the young one.'

'Well, yes, Miss Philippa, of course. But
all that's over now.'

'She's engaged, is she?'

'Well, in a manner, yes; but she doesn't
like it talked about.'

'And you are to marry Miss Agnes?'

'I never said so. I have no right to say
so. I only said that there were things more
unlikely to happen; and you must understand
that even that was said in the strictest confidence. Come, it's getting late, and we are
early risers at Halswater. How is your room?
I hope you think it snug enough.'

'Snug!' said Richard, rolling his hollow eyes about what was certainly a very handsome apartment. 'I feel like Christopher Sly in the play.'

'Or like Mr. Squeers in his Sunday clothes,' replied Mr. Edward, laughing, 'astonished at finding yourself so respectable.'

CHAPTER XXVIII

AN INEXPLICABLE ALARM

THE most prudent and scheming folk cannot make provision for everything, and especially for what they may say or do themselves in a moment of impulse.

For many months Mr. Edward Roscoe had been in expectation of some such meeting as that which had just taken place between himself and his brother. A less confident man would perhaps have rehearsed his own part in it beforehand; but, though he was by no means one to trust to the inspiration of the moment, he had not dreamt of taking such a precaution. He had always been Richard's superior (and, to say truth, had treated him as if he was), and somewhat despised his intelligence. He had not made allowance for the independence of character which the knocking about in the world for years gives to a man who may have had but little of it to start with. He had expected to find him as clay to the hand of the potter, and he had found him rather stiff clay; he foresaw that he should have more trouble with him than he expected, and, on the whole, was sorry he had sent for him. He regretted now that he had given way to the temptation of boasting to him of his own position; his pride of place had caused him, he felt, to be unnecessarily confidential. It was foolish of him to admit, or rather to allow Richard to guess, that he had marriage with Agnes in his eye; for once, moved by impulses of which he was now rather ashamed, he had been both frank and truthful. He had really sent for his brother with the object he had mentioned, directly he had become aware of the contents of Mr. Tremenhere's will; but the wife he had designed for him was not Philippa but Grace. At that time the latter had had no suitor, and it struck Mr. Edward that she could not do better than ally herself with one who would be under his own control, and with whom matters could be made easy. As he remembered Richard, he was a handsome young fellow, not without spirit, though always inclined to lean upon another rather than trust to his own resources; somewhat sentimental in feeling, and very impressionable to female beauty. Fortunately, since Lord Cheribert had stepped into the vacant place, he no longer wanted his brother for this purpose, for indeed he now seemed quite unfitted for it. To his eyes he looked a broken man, worn out by fatigues and ill-health, which had also made him irritable and difficult to deal with. He had, it is true, suffered certain wrongs at his elder brother's hands; but that was long ago; and since Edward had shown a disposition to make amends, it was Richard's duty (as, indeed, he had hinted to him) to forget them, and make himself useful to his patron. In time, and with kind and judicious treatment, this would doubtless come about; and in that case it would not be a matter to be deplored that he had thus made a confidant of him, as respected his own matrimonial designs, from the first.

It would be of immense advantage to him to have at the Hall one whose interests were his own, for he was well aware that, with the exception of its two mistresses, there was no one at Halswater Hall on whose good-will he could rely. Though he had nothing to complain of from Grace herself, he felt that he could hardly count upon her personal regard as of old. Her intimate relations with Mr. Allerton, his declared enemy, forbade it. This was another reason why he was anxious to get her a husband as soon as possible, who would remove her from the scene of his operations. If she had really any tenderness for Lord Cheribert, which he did not doubt, he was confident that, so far as she was concerned, the immense pecuniary loss which her marriage would cause her would weigh with her not a feather; nor from what he knew of Lord Cheribert did he think that if even he was made conscious of that fact it would seriously affect his intentions. The young man was reckless and headstrong, and had always been wont to please himself at any cost; his noble father, of course, would entertain the strongest objections to such a match without the gilding, but the young man's career had been one long opposition to the paternal wishes.

Mr. Allerton's views, if they were adverse, would be of much more consequence, since he enjoyed the confidence of both the young people; but in Mr. Allerton lay Mr. Roscoe's chief hope; it was, he believed, in the lawyer's power to set aside the conditions of Mr.

Tremenhere's will, and if that were effected
he would be satisfied, though in a different
manner from that which he now contem-
plated.

Unconscious of the large share she occupied in Mr. Roscoe's thoughts, and having
nothing in common with them, Grace Tremenhere recommenced her home life (for in
spite of the comparatively short time she
resided there every year, she had always
looked on Halswater as ' home ') much as she
had been wont to pass it, though under
changed conditions.   There was no father
now to saunter about the garden with his
' little fairy,' or to tempt to wander further
afield ; his sedentary habits had hitherto often
prevented her from taking the long walks
over the fells in which her soul delighted, and
which she undertook with perfect fearlessness.
She knew her way, as her sisters said, ' blind-
fold,' and indeed so it almost seemed to their
townbred fancy ; even in the hill fogs, of

which, however, she had had as yet no serious experience, she rarely lost her bearings, and had been termed in consequence by some chance visitor at the inn 'the Maiden of the Mist.' It was curious how much oftener than before her wanderings now took the direction of the inn—not the direct road which ran by the lake side, but some mountain path, or mountain where there was no path, from which in the far distance the white-walled 'Welcome,' set in its emerald dale, could be seen gleaming like a star.

The first snow had not yet fallen on the fells, but the mists were growing more frequent, and Autumn, though there were few leaves to show the mark of her 'fiery finger,' was coming on apace. The air was rich and heavy with the scent of it, and, though not unwholesome to those in health, already perilous to those of feeble lungs. The circumstance was not unwelcome to her, since it afforded her a good excuse for not becoming that mountain guide to their new visitor which her sisters had promised for her. Mr. Richard Roscoe was, for the present at all events, distinctly an invalid; he had a churchyard cough (as his brother humorously termed it), found mountain climbing much too laborious, and the damps of evening injurious. She was sorry for him, for he was of a roving nature, had spent the later years of his life more out of doors than in, and inaction was irksome to him; but just now the companionship of anyone, and especially of a stranger, would have been very obnoxious to her. She preferred to think her own thoughts—vague, and often sad as they were—in the free air of hills, to making polite conversation. It was her custom, after the occupations of the morning, which generally included visits to the sick in the neighbouring hamlet, to dedicate the afternoon to nature in a long ramble with the faithful Rip over the fells. In a few weeks more there would be no rambling of that kind; the hollows of the hills would be filled up with snow, and their summits cold and icebound; but in the meantime she enjoyed her mountain walks immensely. Though she was no poet, and the cataract could not be said to 'haunt her like a passion,' she took great pleasure in the foaming becks, and the steep sheer precipices down which they plunged. Her eye was keen, her foot was sure, and fear was unknown to her. Not seldom had she found the sheep 'crag fast,' and told the shepherd of the danger of his missing charge. Such scenes, such pleasures, were a hundred times more grateful to her than the amusements and dissipations of the town. Her rôle of 'heiress' was singularly unsuited to her, and but for the benefits which, thanks to Mr. Allerton, she was enabled vicariously to diffuse, it gave her no pleasure. All that she had seen and heard since her father's death of the effects of wealth had engendered contempt and dislike of it. It had been the cause of her sisters' disrespect to his memory, and, as she vaguely perceived, of their hostility to one another. Perhaps she had even a presentiment that it might one day prove an obstacle to the dearest though unconfessed desire of her soul.

Although Grace was glad to escape from the threatened companionship of Mr. Richard Roscoe in her walks, his society at times was far from displeasing to her; and indeed, though it could scarcely be called an acquisition, it had for the whole family at Halswater a certain sense of relief. His presence, as in the case of the former visitors at Elm Place, was a restraint upon the hostility with which the two elder sisters unhappily regarded each other, and which seemed to increase day by day. It afforded his brother opportunities of escape from their continuous appeals against each other. For

Grace, too, at least Richard had also an attraction of his own. Independent of the obvious delicacy of his health that claimed her pity, there was a melancholy about him which bespoke her sympathy. She felt sure that some recollection of his past gave him acute mental pain, though he did his best to conceal it, and she had reason to suspect, from a word dropped now and again, that this was caused by the remembrance of another's sufferings. That he had suffered himself from severe privations, he admitted, though he was very disinclined to dwell on them. 'I have had a very hard life, Miss Grace,' he once said to her, but it did not seem to her to have made a hard man of him. She had an instinct that under a rough exterior he carried a tender heart. When she had replied on that occasion, 'And also, from what your brother tells me, a perilous life,' he had answered 'Yes,' then added with a painful smile, 'You must not ask me to detail my adventures : they are nothing to boast of, and would only distress you to hear of them.'

She had an idea that some one dear to him had undergone in his company some shocking experience which it was painful to recall. Even what his brother knew of what he had gone through in his wild and wandering life, and which Edward was rather inclined to depreciate, as is the custom with men of his class (who have often perils enough, but quite of another kind than those of the traveller and the explorer), was sufficient to establish his courage ; his very modesty upon the point corroborated it ; and yet Richard Roscoe exhibited at times an utterly groundless trepidation. It did not need a medical training to understand that this was the consequence of some shock to the nerves. His sleep was disturbed by terrible dreams—a circumstance which it was impossible to conceal from the servants at the cottage. 'Poor Richard is frightened by shadows,' Mr. Roscoe used rather contemptuously to observe, 'though, to do him justice, I believe, by nothing else.'

Just now he was really too much of an invalid for much exertion, and it was difficult to believe, what was nevertheless the fact, that when in health he had possessed thews of steel and nerves of iron. On one occasion, however, it happened that a horse was brought for Mr. Roscoe to 'trot out,' for his own riding. The groom who led it up to the door warned him that in his opinion it was a nasty one, of a bad temper.

'Why do you say that?'

'Well, sir, he has thrown two men in the yard already.'

'Then you had better try him yourself instead of me,' suggested prudent Mr. Edward. The groom mounted, not very willingly, and after a second or two of 'masterly inaction,' the creature sprang into the air with its four legs brought together like those of a chamois on a crag, and cast the man over his head.

'A buck-jumper, by Jingo!' exclaimed the invalid, who, with the ladies, was watching this performance from the porch, and in three strides he was by the horse's side, and had vaulted on his back in a second.

It seemed almost like a miracle performed by a cripple; but still greater was the wonder of the beholders when, as the animal bucked again and again, with his head so low that he looked headless, they saw the rider maintain his seat as though he and his steed were one. In the end the man tired out the horse, who for the time was completely subjugated, and having descended from the saddle in safety, Mr. Richard fainted away. Among the out-door servants at the Hall he became from that moment, what his brother had never been to his *valet-de-chambre*, a hero; and, indeed, the feat made no slight impression even on the ladies. Physically, it did him no good, since for days afterwards he felt the effects of it. One afternoon Grace sacrificed her walk, and took the invalid in her pony-carriage for a drive to the seaside. For this act of kindness he was more than grateful, and as they drove along he became more confidential than he had hitherto permitted himself to be. He spoke of his aimless and broken life in a manner that touched Grace keenly, but with a conviction of its hopelessness that seemed to forbid a word of encouragement.

'I was never much,' he said in his queer fashion, 'and could never have come to much; so after all it don't much matter.'

About his brother's connection with his affairs he was reticent, but he owned that he was under a great obligation to him for having invited him to Halswater. Without it, he averred that he would have had no more chance of mixing with such society

as he had found than of 'getting to heaven'
—a contingency he seemed to consider exceedingly remote. He never spoke of Walter
Sinclair, and Grace did not venture to touch
upon that subject; she shrank from exhibit-
ing her interest in him to one who, from
what Walter had said, had after all been
his father's friend rather than his own.
Once he let fall a congratulatory word
about Lord Cheribert, but upon perceiving
the subject to be unwelcome to his companion immediately dropped it; not, however, without a glance of pleased surprise,
which afterwards recurred to her with significance. He seemed to her somehow to
read her real feelings as regarded the young
lord, and to express his satisfaction that he
had not found favour in her sight; a circumstance probably due to what it was
only too likely he had heard of Lord Cheribert's mode of life. Yet, if so, it was somewhat strange that Mr. Richard Roscoe, of

all men with a past, should be masquerading as Mrs. Grundy. There were things, however, stranger than that about him, as she had presently cause to know.

The proposed limit of their drive was a certain little country town, in the environs of which there was a field, in which, as it happened, a travelling circus had pitched its tent. As they neared it, certain sounds shrilled from within it, which overcame the concert of drums and trumpet without.

'Great heavens!' exclaimed Richard Roscoe, 'did you hear that?'

'I heard some one holloaing,' replied Grace; 'there is some equestrian performance going on; the people are cheering.'

'No, no,' replied her companion, at the same time, to her extreme astonishment, laying his hand upon the reins; 'it is not that; it is something quite different. Would you oblige me by turning back—pray let us go home.'

She assented, of course. The speaker's face was pale, and greatly agitated. The dew even stood out upon his forehead. For the moment she had feared for his reason; but directly the pony's head was turned the vehemence of her companion's manner disappeared. His expression of alarm and, as it had even seemed, of panic, was succeeded by one of exhaustion and distress; he lay back in the vehicle as one reclining in an invalid carriage. They drove a mile or more in total silence.

Then he said: 'Miss Grace, you must think me out of my mind; it is only that something which occurred yonder awoke a very painful association. You have forgiven me for my foolish conduct, I know.'

'There was nothing to forgive in it,' she answered, mustering up a smile.

'It is kind of you to say so; but you are always kind. May I still further trespass upon your good nature by asking you to

say nothing of the—to you doubtless un-
accountable—weakness of which I have been
guilty ?'

She promised silence, of course, and kept
her promise; but it would have been contrary to human nature had not her curiosity
been aroused by the incident. She took some
pains to discover what sort of entertainment
was then going about that part of the
country; but all she gathered was that it
was a circus, consisting of the usual per-
forming steeds, a tribe of wild Indians (probably Irish), and 'the champion huntress
of the Rocky Mountains,' a young lady scan-
tily attired, for that inclement region, in
tights.

CHAPTER XXIX

THE HILL FOG

FOR the next few days after his drive with
Grace, Mr. Richard confined himself to the
cottage, on the plea of indisposition, and
Grace would perhaps have forgotten what
she was nevertheless persuaded had been
its cause, but for a paragraph that happened to meet her eye in the county newspaper. It had the sensational heading of
' Mysterious Attack upon an Indian Chief,'
and described how one of the members of
a travelling circus, taking a Sunday walk on
the hills in the vicinity of the neighbouring
town, had been set upon and severely beaten
by some unknown person.

Robbery could not have been the motive

—indeed there was little beyond a blanket and feathers to steal; and it was the Chief's opinion that nothing less than murder had been intended; he had thought himself lucky to save his scalp.

The paragraph escaped the attention of the other members of the family, and Grace forbore to refer to it, lest the mind of the invalid should be led to revert to a subject it was obviously better he should forget; and the incident made the less impression upon her because of certain circumstances which just now took place in connection with her own affairs. The Tremenhere ladies had not only not been brought up in the strict sect of the Pharisees (notwithstanding the terms of their father's will), but had been left very much to their own devices; they had read, for example, pretty much what they pleased, nor had anyone ever dreamt of forbidding them the daily newspaper. At Halswater (where, however, they did not get it till the next day) it was eagerly perused by all of them, as the link which united them to the outside world.

On a certain afternoon, when Grace took it up as usual in the library, where her sisters were sitting, she found that it was two days old.

'Where is yesterday's newspaper?' she inquired of Agnes.

'It has not come to-day, my darling,' replied her sister.

Her tone, Grace thought, was unusually kind and tender.

'But indeed I saw Philippa with it,' she answered.

'No, my dear,' said Philippa, patting Grace's cheek with her hand, an unwonted mark of sisterly affection in her also, 'that was the old copy. No newspaper came to-day; we shall doubtless get two to-morrow.'

Mr. Roscoe, who had opened the post-bag according to custom, confirmed this statement;

but nevertheless the missing paper never turned up.

The incident made little impression on Grace, but the increased affection in the manner of her sisters, which continued to be manifested to her, did not escape her attention. Even Mr. Edward, who was always paternal in his behaviour to her, seemed to catch from them this epidemic of tenderness.

If there was an exception in the general domestic attitude towards her, it was that of Mr. Richard. Ever since their little adventure together he had seemed to shun her society, but now he appeared absolutely to shrink from it. There was nothing, indeed, of antagonism or dislike in his manner; on the contrary, it seemed rather to arise from an excess of modesty and the sense of his own unworthiness. He seldom spoke to her, but sometimes she caught his eyes fixed upon her with an earnestness that suggested a much closer study of her than she had dreamt of;

but in this too there was nothing inquisitive or impertinent. The expression of his face, as that flush of recognition had shown it to her, was one of tenderness, but also of profound pity. It had nothing of selfishness about it, and yet she felt strangely disinclined to ask its explanation. Even with her sisters she maintained a strict reticence as respected their change of conduct ; for it somehow came into her mind that the continued delay of Lord Cheribert to pay his promised visit was at the bottom of it.

Perhaps they had heard that he did not intend to come at all, and were keeping the news from her, under the mistaken idea that it would be a disappointment that would wring her very heartstrings. If so, this would explain Mr. Richard's sympathy, for, as she knew from his reference to him when they were driving together, he had been informed of her supposed attachment to the young lord. She was too sensible to resent it, since it was obvious that he meant well ; but of course it was disagree-able.

What corroborated Grace's view of this matter was that she noticed more than once, on her entering the room where her sisters and Mr. Roscoe were sitting together, that her arrival caused them to suddenly break off their conversation and start some other topic. If her surmise was correct, this was only to be expected ; but what did astonish her very much was that Mr. Richard was actually taken to task by his brother for not pursuing the same line of conduct adopted by the rest. This came to her knowledge by the merest accident.

She was in her boudoir one afternoon—writing a letter to Mrs. Lindon, who had sent her a pressing invitation to visit her at the seaside—when the two brothers passed under her window. She loved the fresh air, even when it had the bite of winter in it ; but this was not Mr. Roscoe's taste, and from seeing the window open he naturally concluded that she was out of doors. If he had thought otherwise, he would certainly not have said what he did say in her hearing. It was only a scrap of conversation as they went slowly by, and she had no time to make her presence known to them before it was uttered and they had passed by.

'I think you are behaving very foolishly to the girl, Richard. Why can't you treat the matter as we do?'

'Because I can't feel as you do,' was the quiet reply. 'In place of her needing commiseration I think she has had a fortunate escape.'

'Still, for her own sake it would be only natural if you were to show a little sympathy, which some day she would be grateful for, and at all events it is the best way to recommend——' and then the voices died away as the sound of the steps upon the gravel grew faint.

That these words had reference to herself she had no doubt; but their meaning puzzled her. What *could* it matter to Mr. Roscoe that his brother showed no sympathy about a matter concerning which he had no personal knowledge, and what was it that a contrary course of conduct was likely to recommend to her? It never entered into her mind that she should be the centre of any scheme or plot; she had no apprehension of danger of any kind; she was conscious of having aroused no enmity, and indeed had just now rather to complain of an excess of affection than the want of it.

But she did feel the need of sympathy very much; nay more, she suffered from a certain sense of isolation, which had of late grown more and more intolerable. She had never, it is true, had even a school friend; she had been brought up at home, and the home visitors, except perhaps Mrs. Lindon, had never been much more to her than acquaintances. Hitherto this lack of intimates had not troubled her, because she had had no secret to share with them. But now—now—oh, what would she not have given for some loving friend of her own sex to whom to confide the tender hope that lay hid in her heart, and the anxious fears that hemmed it round! Under no circumstances would she have confided it to either of her sisters, nor perhaps at any time, though in her father's lifetime she had not felt herself so much estranged from them, but least of all just now, when the very interest they manifested in her was probably caused by a total misconception of her feelings. She could give no explanation of it, but somehow or other the few words she had just heard fall from the lips of the two brothers intensified this feeling of isolation. It had been her intention, on sitting down to write to Mrs. Lindon, to decline that lady's invitation; her would-be hostess had always been kind to her (as, indeed, she would have been to her sisters had they not rejected her advances); but she felt she had little in common with her, and to pay visits when we are out of heart is a melancholy counterfeit of enjoyment indeed. But now even Mrs. Lindon's roof seemed preferable to that of home. For the present, however, she left the letter unfinished, and since it was still early in the afternoon, started at once for one of her walks over the fells. More than once Grace had found the mere exercise of lung and limb in the open air a tonic for the mind, and seldom had she felt the need of a tonic more than on the present occasion.

There would not be many more such walks for her that year, she knew. Early as it was, the autumn mists were already beginning to rise on Halswater. Upon the south side of it rose precipitous cliffs of friable stone, very apt at that season to descend in considerable volume, like miniature avalanches, into the lake, which made the narrow path that skirted its dark depths not a little dangerous. In clear weather this thin line could be traced to Dale End, the very extremity of the mere, where the 'Fisher's Welcome' stood, with a handful of stone-built cottages about it, and the little church which, but for its tower, might have passed for a cottage too; but now, less than half-way on its course, the path was lost in a fleecy veil, which was not the haze of distance.

More significant still, on the eastward horizon, as far as the eye could range, there was a patch of pure white, which a less experienced person might have taken for cloud; but Grace knew better. It was no cloud, but would endure for months and months to come, and spread and spread till all other peaks were like it—the first snow on the Skiddaw Range. Nearer home there were other signs which a good daleswoman like herself could read. One of them, had she been inclined to nervous fears, might have made her pause. Though the afternoon was fine and all the hills stood out as clear as though cut with the chisel, Blackscale, one of the outpost mountains which stand like sentinels on the seacoast, was half hidden in mist. There is a local proverb,

> When Blackscale has a cap,
> Halse Fell knows full well of that,

the translation of which is that when the mist settles on one it will not be long before it finds the other. And Halse Fell was the very spot whither Grace was bound. It was the highest mountain in the neighbourhood, though not nearly so much of a climb to Halswater folk, who were themselves very highly placed, as it would have been to one starting from the seacoast. Grace herself had often been to the top of it and back in a little over three hours. She did not now intend to scale its summit, though it looked very tempting, but, keeping pretty much to the level to which she had already attained, to circumnavigate it, and, striking over its neck, to descend by a well-known path into Dale End, and so home by the road. Though quite fearless, and confident in her own powers, she was not reckless, and much too wise to run the risk of being caught by a mist on the top of Halse Fell, a picturesque locality made up of precipice alternating with ravine.

Long before Grace reached the proposed turning-point of her journey the sunshine had given place to a grey gloom, which yet was not the garb of evening. The weather looked literally ' dirty,' though she was too little of a sailor, and too much of a gentlewoman, to call it so. Instead of running on ahead of her mistress and investigating the rocks for what Mr. Roscoe, who was cockney to the backbone (and prided himself on it) *would* call sweetmeats (meaning sweetmarts), Rip kept close to her skirts. Rip had never seen a mart, whether sweet or foul, but, when on the hills, he was always buoyed up by the hope of seeing, or at all events of smelling, one. Now, on the contrary, he seemed to be saying to himself, 'No more hunting after these rock carrions. Would it were supper-time and all were well, and my mistress and I safe at home at Halswater!'

It was ridiculous to suppose that a town-bred dog should scent atmospheric dangers upon the mountains of Cumberland; but his spirits had certainly quitted him with inexplicable precipitancy, and every now and then he would give a short impatient bark, which said as plainly as dog could speak, 'Hurry up, unless you want to be up here all night, and perhaps longer.'

This strange conduct of her little companion did not escape Grace's attention, and though she did not understand it it caused her insensibly to quicken her steps. She had rounded Halse Fell, and was just about to leave it for the lower ground, when she suddenly found herself in darkness. The fell had not only put its cap on, it was drawn down over its white face as that other white cap, still more terrible to look upon, covers the features of the poor wretch about to be 'turned off' on the gallows. The suddenness of the thing (for there is nothing so sudden as a hill fog, except a sea fog) gave it, for the moment, quite the air of a catastrophe. To be in cotton-wool is a phrase significant of superfluous comfort; and yet, curiously enough, it seemed to express better than any other the situation in which Grace now found herself, in which there was no comfort at all. She seemed to be wrapped around in that garment which ladies call 'a cloud'—only of a coarse texture and very wet. It was over her eyes and nose and mouth, and rendered everything invisible and deadened every sound.

She could just hear the piercing whine (with half the sharpness taken out of it) of the faithful dog at her feet, exclaiming, 'Now the London fog had come at last, which he had felt in the air for the last ten minutes,' and inquiring, ' What were they to do now?' She didn't know any more than he did. What had happened was beyond her experience. She only knew from hearsay that there was one danger which cragsmen feared above all the rest except the snow-drift, namely the hill fog, and that here it was.

It might clear away in five minutes, and it might last all night. To move would be fatal. Should she take one unconscious turn to left or right, she was well aware that she would lose all her bearings; and yet, from a few feet lower than where she stood now, could she but have seen a hundred yards in front of her, she knew there would be comparative safety. She could no more see a hundred yards, or ten, or five, however, than she could see a hundred miles. Things might have been worse, of course. She might have been at the top of the fell instead of half-way down it. She had been in fogs herself, but not in one like this, nor so far from home. But matters were serious enough as they were.

Though there was no wind of course, the air had become very damp and chill. To keep her head clear, to husband her strength, should a chance of exerting it be given her, and to remain as warm as possible, were the best, and indeed the only, things to be done. Keeping her eyes straight before her, she sat down, and took Rip on her lap. But for its peril, the position was absurd enough; but it was really perilous. Lightly clad as she was, for the convenience of walking, she could hardly survive the consequences of such a night on the open fell.

Moreover, though she had plenty of courage, her previous experience of life unfitted her for such an ordeal. A native of the hills would not have been so depressed by the circumstances in which she had found herself so unexpectedly placed. To a townsman the want of arrangements for lighting the place at night seems always the most serious defect of the country— he misses his gas-lamps more than anything —but night on the mountains, without moon or star, with the sense of having been put in a bed with wet sheets added, is a much more serious matter. The contrast her situation afforded to anything within her experience added vastly to its tragedy. An incident she had once read of a clerk in a Fleet Street bank being sent suddenly on pressing business into Wales, and all but perishing the very next night, through a sprained ankle, on a spur of Snowdon, came into her mind. How frightful the desolation of his position had seemed to him—its unaccustomed loneliness and weird surroundings, and the ever-present consciousness of being cut off from his fellows, in a world utterly unknown to him!

She was now enduring the selfsame pangs.

CHAPTER XXX

RIP FINDS A FRIEND

As the time went by, each minute with the tardiness of an hour, and each decreasing, as she was well aware—for was it not bringing on the night?—her slender stock of hope, it seemed to her that had it not been for the presence of her little dumb companion she must even thus early have given up the fight. But Rip was more frightened even than his mistress, and shivered and moaned, and 'snoozled' his cold nose in her thin cloak, so piteously, that the thought of having something to protect even more helpless than herself quickened her energies. The look-out, however—if such it could be called, where nothing was to be seen: her own hand held up before her was scarcely visible—was gloomy indeed. There had been times of late, when, wretched in her isolation at home, and sickened with suspense, and the unbroken silence of one she loved in secret, death had almost appeared welcome to her! But, as in the fable, now that he seemed to be drawing near to her, she shrank from the King of Terrors.

What would she have given now to be sitting by the fire in her boudoir, even though without much cheerful food for thought! The affection of her sisters might not be of a very genuine kind, but how truly would they pity her could they know of her melancholy position! Mr. Roscoe himself (though there was little 'love lost' between them) would not be unmoved; and Mr. Richard, she was confident, would be something more than sympathetic. If Lord Cheribert could know, too, whether he had thought better of coming to Halswater or not, or as the conduct of her relatives almost led her to suspect, had altered his views in regard to her—what pangs of pity would he not suffer on her account! how furious he would be with Fate itself, that had so cruelly treated her! He would be as angry with the mountains, if she should perish among them, as King Xerxes. And above all, what would Walter say? There was no reserve in her thoughts about him now; why should there be, when in all probability they were her last thoughts? She was saying good-bye to Walter though he knew it not, and nobody would ever know it.

She had closed her eyes, as people often do when their thoughts are very sad and deep, but opened them quickly as the dog gave a sharp quick bark. She looked up, and, lo! there was a small clear space in front of them; it was very limited, and bore the same sort of ratio to the blinding mist about them as the space swept for a few slides on a frozen lake where all else is covered with snow; but space there was, so that she could see her way

down to the Col—the top of the pass that led
to Dale End. She strove to rise to her feet,
but it was very difficult; her limbs were stiff
and numb to a degree that she had not suspected; it seemed to her that she was already
half-way to death.

The dog had leapt from her arms and
run forwards, as if rejoicing at its new-found
liberty, and she feebly tottered after it. With
every step she felt strength and hope returning to her ; a few more yards, and she knew
that, if her present course could only be
maintained, safety, or what in comparison
would be safety—and swift as the thought of
it the mist closed round her again like a
curtain, and she dared not move one step.
Her position was locally only a little better
than it had been, and in one respect a hundred
times worse, for she had lost her little companion. In vain she uttered his name in a tone
of passionate entreaty such as she would have
thought it impossible to use towards a dumb

animal; it might even be that he did not recognise her voice, or, what was more likely, it could not pierce the wool-like atmosphere that hid her from even his sharp eyes. How idle were all those stories of canine instinct, when the poor animal was thus unable to rejoin her though separated by such a little space! That he already yearned to do so she was convinced; and notwithstanding her own miserable condition, she felt a tender pity for the little creature deprived of its human friend. It would, indeed, probably survive when she should have perished, but it would never forget its mistress, or find a new one to fill her place; she loved the dog, not only for its own sake but for another's.

It was amazing how the loss of this little link to the world of life increased her sense of loneliness and despair. After her late experience, she dared not sit down again, and indeed even yet she had not quite recovered the use of her limbs; she stood, with her arms folded to keep warmth in them, and her eyes fixed before her, in feeble hope that some current of wind, as before, might lift the veil in front of her.

Then suddenly she heard the dog bark. The very sound was cheering to her, but the nature of the sound was infinitely more inspiriting ; for notwithstanding the thickness of the atmosphere, which choked it, and made it seem a far greater distance from her than the animal really was, she recognised in it an unmistakable note of joy. Rip had found something—perhaps even somebody—the meeting with which had transported him with pleasure. She knew Rip's bark too well to doubt it ; and she could almost imagine the little creature jumping and bounding as it gave forth those notes of glee.

They were not only repeated but continuous, and with an irresistible impulse she pushed through the wall of mist, which parted and closed like water behind the hand in their direction. She could see nothing, but they sounded nearer and nearer, and presently the dog himself sprang out of the fleecy veil in joyous welcome, and then sprang back again.

She followed, and presently the figure of a man loomed up before her.

'Good Heavens! it *is* Miss Grace!' he cried.

She answered nothing; she had recognised him, but the shock of joy was too much for her overtaxed energies, and she fell fainting into Walter Sinclair's arms.

Was it night and a dream? she wondered, when, having presently come to herself, she found the man, on whom her thoughts had dwelt so long and tenderly, beside her in that desolate place. How *could* he have got there? Amazing, however, as was the circumstance, it was no time for asking questions. For the moment, indeed, her vocal powers seemed to have deserted her with all the rest. Walter, however, had a flask of sherry in his pocket, and administered to her some of its contents, with instantaneous effect. How strange it is that there are persons, otherwise in their right minds, who (because some people are drunkards) persuade themselves that under no possible circumstances can wine be beneficial to anybody! To this shivering and nerve-shaken girl it gave new life, and instead of 'stealing away her brains' recovered them for her.

She wasted no time in congratulations—not unconscious, perhaps, that there had been enough of them already, and warm ones, upon the gentleman's part; it had been so necessary, you see, to preserve her circulation—but showed her practical good sense at once by the inquiry:

'You came up from Dale End, I suppose.'

'Yes; I was bound for the Start valley; and on the Mare's Back here, as they call it, I believe, the fog caught me. As I had noticed there was a precipice on either side, I thought it best to stay where I was; I was getting a little tired of waiting when Rip found me. Now, as it seems to me, I could wait for ever quite patiently.'

Grace took no notice of this philosophic reflection.

'It is the most dangerous pass in the district—that is, to the stranger,' she observed, 'but to one who knows the bearings, if one could only find them——'

'I have a pocket-compass,' he interrupted; 'happily (or I should not have found you), it was of no use to me, but perhaps you can make something of it.'

It was much too dark for the face of the little instrument to be discerned, but Walter had some cigar-lights (there are some people, again, who say that smoking is pernicious, but they are quite mad), and by help of one Grace made out their position.

'We are facing due east, and must keep straight on,' she said with confidence.

'In that case you must let me go first,' he answered quietly, 'for, without presuming to doubt your information, it seems to me, so far as I have been able to keep the direction in my mind, that will lead us over the left-hand precipice.'

'No doubt,' she replied, smiling; 'and to turn back would lead us over the right-hand one. You have an admirable memory, but you are not a dalesman, Mr. Sinclair.'

It was amazing how the speaker's spirits had come back to her. She spoke almost as if she were already out of her difficulties, whereas apparently all that had happened was a slight improvement in the position. It was as though the defenders of some beleaguered city had received an unexpected reinforcement, which was nevertheless much too weak to enable them to make a sally, so that they were beleaguered still.

'I am in your hands, of course,' said Walter. This was not quite a correct statement, for Grace was in *his* hands ; or rather her hand was in one of his, while his other arm encircled her waist ; it was so important, you see, that they should not get separated in the fog ; even poor little Rip seemed to understand this, and stuck almost as close to them as they were to one another. 'I will do exactly as you please ; but it seems to me that we had better wait here, where we are pretty comfortable, till the fog lifts and shows us where we are going.'

'Unless the wind rises the fog will not lift,' said Grace. 'At present there is still daylight somewhere, if we can only get to it.'

'Eastward ho, then, with all my heart!' exclaimed Walter.

Then they moved forward very slowly, one foot at a time, like folks in the dark on a broad landing feeling for the stair. After a few steps they both nearly came to grief over a little cairn of stones.

'Thank Heaven, we have found it!' exclaimed Grace delightedly.

'That heap of stones! You are thankful for small mercies,' observed her companion, laughing, 'for it almost tripped us up. And, by-the-by, there are plenty more of them; I remember seeing thirty or forty of them at least, so pray be careful.'

'These little cairns are landmarks,' said Grace earnestly. 'I would rather have found one of them than a handful of diamonds. They are placed on this dangerous spot for the very purpose of assisting persons in the same plight as ourselves to find their way. With ordinary caution we ought now to get to Dale End in safety. Again I say "Thank Heaven!"'

'You must forgive me, dear Miss Grace, because selfishness is man's nature, for not echoing that sentiment,' said Walter softly. 'I shall never be so happy in my life, I fear, as when we were lost upon the hills together.'

'It was certainly fortunate for both of us that we found one another,' observed Grace with a provoking simplicity. 'It would never have happened but for dear little Rip. How glad he was to see you! as, indeed, he ought to be.'

'But not one half so glad as I was to see him. I was thinking of you the very moment before I heard the dog's cheery bark.'

'That is strange indeed,' said Grace, who omitted to add that within a few minutes of their meeting she herself had been thinking of *him*.

'And yet not so very strange,' he continued softly, 'since I have thought of little else for the last three days, ever since I have been at Dale End.'

'Three days!' she replied, in a tone of involuntary reproach. 'And why did you not let us know at Halswater how near you were to us?'

There was a long silence; Grace could

not see her companion's face, but she knew it was troubled by some grave emotion.

'I did not like,' he answered presently, in a tone of profound sadness, 'to visit, so soon at least, what I was well convinced would be a house of mourning.'

'A house of mourning!' she repeated wonderingly. 'Nothing has happened, so far as I am aware of.'

'What! Is it possible you do not know? Does it, then, fall to my lot, who would give my life to save you from a single sorrow, to be the bearer of such evil tidings?'

'Great Heavens, do not keep me in suspense, Mr. Sinclair! Is there bad news?'— her voice trembled, her heart grew sick, as she remembered how she had suspected something was kept back from her at the Hall, and it was borne in upon her what that something must be — 'Oh, do not tell me that anything has happened to Lord Cheribert!'

'Then I must hold my tongue,' was the sad rejoinder.

'Is he—is he *dead*?' she gasped.

Walter Sinclair bowed his head, as though the man they spoke of lay beside them in his coffin.

'Yes; he was thrown from his horse in the steeplechase and killed on the spot.'

Grace burst into a passion of tears. 'He said it would be his last race,' she sobbed, 'but how little did he think of it in *this* way! What a future seemed to lie before him! And how worthy he would have been of it! He had an honest and a noble heart.'

Walter Sinclair removed his hat; he seemed to be listening to a eulogy delivered at the grave-side, to every word of which he was assenting.

'He had not an enemy in the world,' she went on, unconscious of a listener, 'but only those who knew him knew his worth. But for money—the having too much of it, and then the having too little of it, and the company among whom it threw him—he would have been a nobler and a better man. He lost his life through it. Dead, and so young! Good Heavens, it is terrible!'

She was still sobbing; her frame was strangely agitated. It was no other motive than sheer fear of her falling that now caused Sinclair to place his arm around her.

She shook herself free of him with a sort of frantic energy.

'No!' she cried, 'I will walk alone.'

He was amazed, for she had not hitherto rejected similar assistance; he could not guess, of course, that she was rejecting it now out of respect for the dead man's memory. The young lord had loved her with his whole heart, she knew, though she had not returned his love; and just now, with the tidings of his death knelling in her ears, she would not wrong him by accepting another's love.

CHAPTER XXXI

HAND IN HAND

' SWIFT as thought,' we say, and yet how little we picture to ourselves not only the immense rapidity with which it travels, but the amazing variety of the subjects with which it deals. In one instant we are communing with our Creator, in the next we are colloguing (an Irish term, but very appropriate) with the Enemy of Mankind. The Curse cuts short the Prayer, or (though not so frequently) *vice versâ*. In a flash we have reached heaven, and sounded the depths of hell. That every word which a man speaks shall one day be cast up against him is credible enough, but that every thought of our hearts shall be made known is a statement too tremendous for the human mind to grasp. If we knew what everybody else was thinking about we should probably hold very little communication with our fellow-creatures; they would be boycotted; we should say to ourselves, 'We really cannot speak to such people. What a mercy it is we don't belong to them.' Even into a young girl's mind there intrude, I suppose, occasionally strange thoughts, things which they had rather not— *much* rather not—utter. As for men, if any man says that he has never been frightened by his own thoughts, he is either a fool, who never thinks, or a liar.

Within the last half-hour the brain of Grace Tremenhere had been busier than it had ever been before within the same period of time. There had been occasions—on that of the fire in the theatre, for example, or that of the death of her father—when she had thought more deeply, and even more vividly; but the thoughts that had crowded into her mind of late had been more various as well as enthralling. They had, in truth, exhausted her almost as much as the physical trials she had undergone. She had looked Death in the face, and said good-bye to Love and Life. And having found both again, she was dissatisfied with them, because the Friendship she had prized so much was now no more. It did not occur to her that if Lord Cheribert had lived, his pertinacity and perseverance, which she never could have rewarded as he wished, would have made both her and him very unhappy; she lamented his death, and the manner of it, beyond measure, chiefly because it had cut him off from the new and nobler course of life he had proposed to himself, but also, no doubt, because he had been her lover. Walter Sinclair, very unjustly, was now suffering from the misfortune that had befallen his rival; it seemed to Grace a disloyalty to the dead man, whose grave had but just closed over him, to let her heart go forth to meet that of the living man she loved, as it longed to do. Nevertheless, the patience and gentleness with which he bore her marked change of manner and her frigid silence presently moved her to pity. As they advanced cautiously from one cairn to another—for all was still wrapped in mist —she forced herself to talk to him a little.

'How strange, indeed, that we should have met here, and under such different circumstances from those under which we parted, Mr. Sinclair!'

An innocent observation enough; but it is one of the disadvantages of compulsory conversation that even the platitudes we use as soon as they have left our lips seem to have some embarrassing significance. Directly she had uttered the words she felt that they might be referred to moral and not material change, the latter of which was of course what she had had in her mind. She almost seemed to herself to have been saying, 'At that time we did not understand one another, did we?' and felt the colour, which fortunately he could not see, flame up in her cheek as she waited for his reply.

'The place is different, indeed,' he answered gently, 'but as to the circumstances, alas! I see little change in them. What does it matter whether a river or a ravine separates a man from the place where he would be, when both are alike impassable?'

'I do not understand you,' she murmured.

'It is like enough,' was the quiet rejoinder. ' My conduct now appears unintelligible even to myself. I see that it has angered you, and no wonder; you must have thought me mad.'

'No.' Even a monosyllable may have tenderness in it, but this had none. She would give him no encouragement—just now —but, on the other hand, she would not affect to misunderstand him; above all, she would not repulse him as she had once done

—a cruelty of which she had so bitterly repented.

'Then that must be owing to your kindness of heart,' he continued, 'which makes allowances for everybody. If you had known what I have gone through, it would, I venture to think, have not been so great an exercise of charity; but then you have not known. If I promise you that it will be the last time that I shall ever refer to it, and that to-day will be the last day that you will ever see me, may I tell it you, Miss Grace?'

'You may tell it me,' she answered softly.

'Then my excuse is that from the first moment I ever saw you I loved you. When I remember who you are, and what I am, it seems the confession of a madman; but it is the truth. You must consider from whence I came; a place where all social gulfs that sever man from woman are passable or can be bridged over; nor, indeed, was I at that time aware of the depth of that gulf, which then as now separates you from me ; under the shelter of your roof I got to recognise it ; though too late for my own peace of mind. You will bear me witness that when I took leave of you I dropped no hint of this. My admiration I could not conceal, but I hid my love in my breast, as the Spartan boy his fox, I never betrayed the torture it caused me. Like him, I was too proud to speak ; for though, like my poor father before me, I have been a hunter, a fortune-hunter I could never be.'

Grace was about to speak, but he stopped her with a gentle movement of his hand. 'You were going to ask me doubtless: " But since you were so wisely resolved, why did you put yourself voluntarily in the way of temptation by coming up to Halswater ? " I may honestly say that Mr. Allerton is partly to blame for this ; he had heard of my intention to visit Cumberland, and pressed me to put it into execution that he might have some information on which he could rely as to how matters were going on with you and yours. He had no suspicion of my own weakness; if I had told him of it, he would have said, kindly disposed though he is towards me, "Do not set your affection on the moon, young man," and he would have been quite right. Nevertheless, what also urged me to take this step was, I admit, my own mad folly; like the moth that seeks the flame in which it is doomed to shrivel, I could not resist the attraction of it. Nevertheless, I exercised some control over myself; when I said that I did not come to the Hall because of the sorrow in which I knew it would be plunged by reason of Lord Cheribert's death, it was not the whole truth; prudence also held me back—a mere selfish prudence, which whispered that ill as it was to encourage an illusion, it would be worse to have it shattered by one before whom my whole soul bowed in reverence. Perhaps but for this chance interview I should never have seen you, for I was well aware of the danger of meeting you face to face; I knew that I might forget the gulf that circumstances have fixed between us.'

'Do you mean my money?'

She spoke coldly, even contemptuously; but there was an undercurrent in her tone that freed it from offence; he felt that the contempt was not for him.

'That is, of course, a very important matter.'

'Not to me, Mr. Sinclair; nor, unless I have much mistaken your character, to you. As a matter of fact, however,' here she smiled a little, 'the gulf you speak of is neither so deep nor so wide as you imagine. It is unnecessary to discuss the question, which would have no attraction for me; Mr. Allerton would have put you in possession of all such details had you asked him.'

'Good Heavens, but how *could* I ask

him! Such an idea never crossed my mind; nor if it had should I have dared to utter it. What would he have thought of me? He has at present a better opinion of me than I deserve, but in that case he would have had a far worse one.'

'I suppose so; I quite see your difficulty,' she answered serenely; 'he would have taken a lawyer's view, and misunderstood you.'

'And you do *not* misunderstand me?' he answered with tender earnestness, 'and you say the gulf is not so deep nor wide between us as I had imagined. Is it possible, dare I ask is it possible, that you would give me— no, lend me—your hand to help me across it? Or, if that is too much, would you mind saying that you are not angry with me?'

'I am certainly not angry with you, Mr. Sinclair.'

'Nor even displeased that you have met me? That is all that I ask just now. It may seem a small thing to you—in that lies my hope—but it would be such a great thing to me. Are you not displeased?'

'I am not displeased with Rip for finding you: that is as much as you can expect me to say, I think,' she answered softly.

'It is more than I dared to hope for,' he answered rapturously. 'What a good dog it is! what a *dear* dog!'

'He is not, however, exactly a St. Bernard,' answered his mistress, smiling; 'the discovery of what we call in Lakeland "the Smoored" is not, I think, the calling that best suits him. The poor little creature seems afraid of putting one paw before another, and sticks to my skirts like a leech.'

'In my opinion that is another proof of his sagacity,' observed her companion. 'How can he do better than stop where he is?'

'At all events it behoves *us* to do better,' returned the young lady; she had fortunately recovered the use of her wits at the very time when the young gentleman seemed to have taken leave of them. 'This is the last cairn, if I have counted rightly, and the mist is as thick as ever, but we have now only to keep on descending; there is nothing to break our necks between here and Dale End.'

For the moment she had forgotten her late peril, and even the evil tidings that had so saddened her: her heart had found what it had so long sought for, though her tongue had not confessed it. The sunshine that was wanting without was resplendent within. Though their way was not slippery, at one place Walter was moved to hold out his hand to help her; she took it, and somehow it didn't seem worth while to let go of it, till they reached the level ground; she might possibly have retained it even then, but the fog was no longer so thick, and it struck her that since objects began to be visible to them they might be visible to others.

CHAPTER XXXII

NEW LIFE

By the time they reached the 'Angler's Rest the sky had only the dull hue of an autumn evening, though the hills were hidden in impenetrable cloud, which Grace shuddered to think might have been her pall.

The landlord, Jack Atkinson, who came out to greet them, exclaimed, ' 'Tis lucky, miss, you were not taking your usual walk over the fells to-day.' He took it for granted she had come by the road. She did not think it necessary to enlighten him on that point: there was gossip even at Dale End, and it would not have been pleasant to make her late adventure the food for it. It struck her, moreover, that her association with her present companion would have to be accounted for. 'Mr. Sinclair is an old friend of our family,' she said, in as indifferent a tone as she could command. 'I hope you are treating him well at the "Rest," Mr. Atkinson.'

'Well, indeed I hope so, miss; though I didn't know as he was a friend of the Hall folk.' And he looked at Sinclair with some surprise. No doubt it seemed curious to him that his guest should have stayed at the inn so long without referring to that circumstance. Sinclair had no such misgivings, and was, indeed, not thinking of his host at all. Men in love are so reckless.

'You look white and tired, Miss Grace,' said the landlord; 'let me have the dogcart out and take you home on wheels.'

'A very good notion!' exclaimed Walter; 'permit me to have the pleasure of driving you, Miss Tremenhere.'

'Thank you very much, Mr. Sinclair,' said Grace politely, 'but I prefer to trust myself to Mr. Atkinson, if he will be so good. His horse is spirited, and the road a bad one, and he knows them both.'

She flattered herself (as is generally the case when we do something disagreeable to another in hopes of some material benefit) that she had effected quite a master-stroke of policy; Atkinson would, she thought, perceive in this preference for his company how indifferent to her was that of Mr. Sinclair. Unhappily, the expression of Walter's face showed that he was very far from indifferent to this arrangement.

'Sorry to cut you out, sir,' said the landlord, with a broad grin, ' but the lady's commands must be obeyed,' and off he went to fetch the cart.

'How could you be so cruel!' exclaimed Walter, with a melancholy sigh.

'How could you be so foolish!' returned Grace, with indignation—not, however, very genuine, for she already felt pity for his disappointment, as indeed she did for her own—'Do you wish to set all these people talking?'

'Oh, I see,' interrupted the young man, with eager, if somewhat tardy, intelligence.

'Not that there is anything really to talk *about*,' continued Grace (which made him all gloom again), 'but country gossip is so easily excited. I shall tell my sisters, of course, that you are here, and under what circumstances I have met you. And I dare say your friend Mr. Roscoe will bring you an invitation from them to dine with us.'

She could not resist that little dig about Mr. Roscoe, for whom he had always shown a respect which she considered beyond that gentleman's deserts.

'I don't know whether I shall accept his invitation,' answered Walter, with a smile that belied his words.

'Well, that is just as you please.' The

landlord now brought out the dogcart, and Walter helped her into it. 'His brother, Mr. Richard, whom you said was a friend of your father's, is now staying with us, which will doubtless be an attraction to you. *Au revoir*, Mr. Sinclair.'

It was really an excellent piece of acting, but it was a mistake to use the French phrase, which the wily proprietor of the 'Angler's Rest' at once set down as part of a secret code of signals established between the young people.

'Seems disappointed like, don't he, miss?' he observed with confidential slyness, as they left her melancholy cavalier behind them; then, perceiving his remark was unappreciated, continued in a less personal vein, 'Thinks he could have driven the horse hisself as well as I can, no doubt. Them Londoners has such a conceit of theirselves. Not, however, as I reckon as Mr. Sinclair is a reglar Londoner, though he came from London?'

'I believe not,' said Grace, seeing a reply was evidently expected; 'he is a friend of Mr. Roscoe's, who can doubtless tell you all about him.'

'And that wouldn't be much, I reckon, neither,' laughed the innkeeper. 'He ain't much given to talk, ain't Mr. Roscoe. Got his brother with him at the Hall, I understand; looks poorly, don't he? And yet he has been a good sportsman in his time, I warrant; not like Mr. Edward.'

Grace began to be sorry, for more reasons than one, that she had favoured Mr. Atkinson at the expense of his rival. The man's tongue ran like a mill-wheel in flood time: and she trembled to think how it might run upon her own affairs as well as those of her belongings. There was nothing, she now felt, that could separate her from Walter; but she did not wish that matter to be taken for granted, or to reach the ears of her relatives by any outside channel. She had lived so much out of the world, that the lively interest which the generality of mankind take in other people's affairs was unknown to her. Perhaps, too, she didn't make allowance for the fact that other people who live out of the world (as at Dale End) never lose an opportunity of hearing something of it, from those they imagine to be possessed of the information. She thought it more dignified as well as discreet to remain silent; but even that, as it turned out, afforded no security.

'Sad thing that about Lord Cheribert at the steeplechase, the other day, was it not, miss?' continued her companion after a short pause. He was really flattered by the preference the young lady had shown him (for he had an honest admiration for her), and thought it, perhaps, part of his duty (as, alas! so many other folks do) to 'make conversation.' 'Mr. Sinclair told me as he knew something of him. Broke his neck in a moment, he did, and didn't suffer like young Harris of Fell Foot, as injured his spine—that is *some* comfort.'

'It was a very, very shocking thing,' murmured Grace, sick and shivering.

'Very much so; though, to be sure, if all tales are true, his lordship was a wild 'un. Ran through half a dozen fortunes, they tell me, by help of the Jews—I mean money-lenders.'

The last words were spoken in an apologetic tone, and the ruddy and weather-worn face of the honest publican as he uttered them became a lively purple. He was naturally loquacious, as an innkeeper should be, and, like the pitcher that goes often to the well, he sometimes got into trouble through it; but it seemed to him that he had never come to such utter grief as on the present occasion. It was only lately that some hint of the late owner of Halswater Hall having belonged to the Jewish persuasion had percolated to Dale End; but it had got there, somehow, and given a new life to its little commnnity as a topic of conversation; in the kitchen of the 'Anglcr's Rest' (for that humble hostelry had no bar-room), Mr. Atkinson had found it most agreeable and provocative of thirst; but that he should have made such a slip as to allude to Jews in the presence of Miss Grace, whom he pictured to himself as sensitive upon the matter as though if her parent had been hung she would have been to an allusion to a rope, filled him with remorse and horror.

Grace knew nothing of the cause, but hailed with gratitude the silence that fell upon her companion in consequence, and endured till they reached the Hall gates. Here she dismissed and recompensed him, and entered the long avenue that led to the house on foot. How different were her feelings from those with which she had left home a few hours before! What experiences had she since gone through! What fears, what sorrows, what delights! How changed, too, was her material position, for had she not found—never, never to be lost again—the beloved of her heart! Her isolation was over; though the winter was about to fall on things without, with her 'all was May from head to heel.' The splendours of her home had hitherto had small attraction for her, but it now seemed a bower of delight. Her path for life would for the future be strewed with flowers.

It is well for us that, now and then, we should have such day-dreams, however sad may be the awakening from them. If we poor mortals could look into the future the shadow of things-to-be would quench all our sunshine. If to Grace Tremenhere the events that were about to happen to her and hers could have been foretold as they were fabled to be of old, the gloom of evening that was now falling around her would have worn the darkness of midnight, and the evening moon would have risen above her as red as blood.

But to her mind's eye all that was not already peace was promise. The troubles of the past—for the moment even her sorrow for the dead—were forgotten. As her eye caught the figure of Mr. Richard coming down the avenue, it reminded her, indeed, of the conversation she had overheard before setting out on her walk between him and his brother, but without recalling the disagreeable sensations it had cost her; she knew no more of what it meant than before, but its mystery no longer troubled her. Love filled her heart and left no room for trouble.

Mr. Richard had been walking rapidly, but on catching sight of her came on more slowly, as though there was no longer need for haste.

'I am so glad to see you safe at home, Miss Grace,' he said with nervous eagerness; ' the boatmen told me that the mist upon the hills was very thick, and I feared you had gone that way.'

'I hope I have not alarmed my sisters,' she returned evasively.

'No, they knew nothing of it, and indeed I have been pacing up and down here to avoid their notice; I have been very much distressed indeed.'

His countenance corroborated his words; it was pale and agitated with nervous twitchings, and his hollow eyes expressed the anxiety that had not yet quitted them.

'You are very kind,' answered Grace gently; 'but here I am, you see, safe and sound. It strikes me that you are running some risk yourself, Mr. Richard, in being out so late in the dewy air after your recent illness.'

'I! What does *that* signify?' he answered. His tone had a contemptuous bitterness which seemed to invite comment; but some instinct warned her to take no notice of it.

'You should take more care of yourself,' she replied quietly. 'And as to fears on other people's account,' she added with a smile, 'we should not give way to them. Even in our own case how idle are often even our worst apprehensions, which nevertheless cause half the unhappiness of our lives!'

It was not always that Grace took such cheerful and sensible views of things, but just now she was looking at life through those windows which love paints rose-colour.

'That is perhaps true,' returned her companion, but with a deep-drawn sigh, and regarding her with a look of tenderest pity; 'but how often, again, is our heart at its lightest on the eve of sorrow, as the bird sings its blithest, unconscious that the hawk is hovering over it.'

'That is what our Cumberland folk call being "fey,"' answered Grace, with a forced smile; she knew to what the other was referring; the tidings of the death of her supposed lover, of which he of course imagined her to be still ignorant. She was certainly not called upon to enlighten him upon the point, but she felt reproved at her own momentary forgetfulness of the calamity, which his words seemed to imply.

'I have some good news for you, Mr. Richard,' she continued, eager to change the subject for another, even though it was not one she would otherwise have been willing to speak of with a comparative stranger; 'Mr. Walter Sinclair, whose father was, I understand, one of your oldest friends, is staying at Dale End.'

'Indeed! Walter Sinclair!' he replied with interest. 'I should greatly like to see him—indeed it is absolutely necessary that I should do so,' he added as if with an afterthought.

'Then nothing can be easier. He is already a friend of the family, you know, and especially of your brother.'

This was another master-stroke of policy of our heroine's: let us not blame her for it, but only hope it will prove more successful than her last; it is only natural that the weaker sex should employ their little subtleties, which have, after all, nothing of hypocrisy about them. Her design was—though she had fairly made up her mind that no earthly power should keep her and Walter sundered—that Mr. Roscoe should himself be made to invite him to the cottage. O joy!—but we must dissemble, for the present at least, for sister Agnes is standing at the front door awaiting us, unbonneted, but with a warm shawl thrown round her shoulders, for the air is chill.

'My dearest Grace, how late you are! We were getting to be quite anxious about you. I am told that there is quite a fog upon the fells.'

CHAPTER XXXIII

POOR DICK

IT was necessary, of course, that Grace should tell her sisters of her meeting with Walter Sinclair on the fells, and also of the sad tidings he had brought her. As it happened, though it would have shocked her to have foreseen any such effect in it, the latter communication greatly assisted her in the more delicate revelation she had to make to them concerning her relations with Walter, and indeed almost did away with the necessity of making it at all. The way in which she spoke of Lord Cheribert's death, though she did so with what was evidently the most genuine and heartfelt sorrow, yet convinced them that they had been in error in supposing that she had loved him ; while the manner in which she referred to Walter convinced them of where her affections had been really placed. This was a satisfaction to both of them, for in their eyes Grace stood in the way of neither of them (whatever Mr. Roscoe might think to the contrary) as they did in that of one another, and they were really as fond of her as it was in their natures to be. They had the turn for match-making common to their sex, and now that Lord Cheribert was gone (though they would have greatly preferred him for a brother-in-law) they were well content (over and above the fact that it would be to their pecuniary advantage) that Walter Sinclair had found favour in their sister's eyes.

'Of course we will have him here,' said Agnes kindly, when the three ladies were alone together after dinner ; 'he might almost as well be in London as at Dale End ; Mr. Roscoe shall invite him to the Cottage, where there is plenty of accommodation for another guest; and that, you know, will settle the matter, so there will be no more room for misunderstanding on anybody's part.'

'There is no chance of any misunderstanding between Walter and myself,' said Grace rather dryly, and with a little flush.

'Which is as much as to say,' observed Philippa, laughing, 'that you two young people have arranged your own affairs together, and are quite independent of the interference of anybody; but nobody,' and here she patted Grace's cheek with her fan, 'is going to interfere, my dear, so you need not become a fretful porcupine all of a sudden and shoot your quills at us.'

'I am sure that Mr. Roscoe, for one, will be certainly glad to hear of the matter,' remarked Agnes gravely.

'And so am I,' put in Philippa quickly; neither sister could ever confess their acquaintance with Mr. Roscoe's views and opinions without the other claiming to have an equal knowledge of them.

'He always liked Mr. Sinclair,' continued Agnes, ignoring the interruption, 'and the circumstance that his father was such a friend of the young man's father, though unimportant in itself, serves to knit the whole thing together very pleasantly.'

In this, however, Agnes was not altogether correct, to judge by a conversation which was at that very moment going on in the smoking-room between the two brothers. Perhaps it was only by contrast with the good spirits of the rest, but Mr. Richard had been even more silent and gloomy than usual during dinner, and had confined his conversation chiefly to monosyllables; even under the consolation of tobacco he bore a very depressed and melancholy air.

'I am really very sorry for you, Dick,' said his brother in a sympathetic tone very unusual to him; 'I am grieved to see you taking your disappointment so to heart, but you must see as plainly as I do that the advice I gave to you this morning was thrown away. Matters have taken quite a different turn—indeed we were going altogether upon false ground—and we shall now have to give the whole thing up.' Richard groaned, and put his hand before his eyes, as if to shield them from the other's gaze. ' Upon my life I'm ashamed of you, Dick,' the other went on disdainfully, ' that a man of your experience of life should take on so about a girl, as if there was only one in the world.'

' There is only one in the world for me,' returned Richard passionately.

' Then you will be so good as to consider her *out* of the world,' observed the other peremptorily, ' as dead as Cheribert ; she is dead to you from this moment, and there's an end of it. I will just show you how the matter stands.'

'It is unnecessary,' replied Richard in hoarse low tones.

'Never mind, I'll state the case, so that there shall be no more mistakes about it.' He stood up with a huge cigar in his mouth and his back to the fire (as old Josh used to stand when he was setting *him* to rights), while his brother sucked at his pipe, with his eyes fixed on the carpet. 'We must have the girl married to somebody, and as soon as possible. When Cheribert broke his neck I thought there was a good chance for you, and, as you know, gave you my best advice how to take advantage of it. It would have been more agreeable to me, of course, that you should have had her than anyone else; but it seems the young lady had already made her choice of a man that was alive and well.' He put the last word in with a slight stress upon it, as though he would have said, 'not a fellow like you, with one leg in the grave.' 'That being so, your hope is gone; we—or I, if you prefer plain speaking, and I don't see why there should be any concealment about the matter—cannot afford to wait any longer for the chapter of accidents, which, indeed, is much more likely to turn out against you than in your favour, and I mean to bring things to a head as soon as possible. Sinclair will be here to-morrow, under this very roof, and here he will stay until they are married. That is as sure as death. Come, be a reasonable man; you must surely know that you have not a shadow of a chance against him.'

'I know it,' answered the other despairingly, 'and if I *had* a chance I would not take it—not against *him*.'

'Well, I care nothing about the sentimental aspects of the question, but I am glad, at all events, you have arrived at such a sensible conclusion.'

'I have got a letter for him,' went on Richard gloomily, and like one speaking to himself rather than to another, 'entrusted to my hands by his father only a few hours before he was murdered.'

'Murdered, was he?' said Edward with a little start, and some show of interest. 'How did that come about?'

'It is a shocking story, and I cannot tell it you just now,' replied the other, again placing his hands before his eyes with a shudder, as though he would have shut out some terrible scene. 'But when we parted he gave me a little packet for his son which he said was of great importance.'

'And what was in it?'

'It was sealed up; but if it had not been so I should not have dreamt of prying into poor Sinclair's secrets. It was a sacred trust.'

'Well, you've still got it, I suppose?'

'Yes, but not here. I did not like to carry it about with me in my wild and wandering life, but left it in safe custody with one on whom I could rely.'

'In America?'

'Yes. I am ashamed to say that when I got your summons I forgot all about the packet. Not, perhaps, that I should have sent for it in any case, since the lad whom it concerned was more likely to be there than here. But now, of course, I shall send for it at once.'

'Quite right. But, if you will be guided by me, I would say nothing about it till it comes.'

'Why not?' inquired Richard, looking up at his brother with a quick suspicious glance.

'Well, if it happens to be lost, you see, it will be a great disappointment to him, for which he will naturally blame you. If he gets it, well and good; and if he does not get it, and if he does not know of it, it will not trouble him.'

'I have already told Miss Grace that I have been entrusted with it.'

'That is as good—or bad—as telling *him*,' replied the other sharply; 'it is amazing to me how a man who knows that he is naturally indiscreet should not keep a better guard over his tongue.'

'Or, before speaking, consult some shrewd adviser who has no interest of his own to serve,' observed Richard dryly.

'That, of course, would be better still,' was the cool rejoinder. 'I think you must admit that the person to whom you refer has managed matters more successfully for you of late than you ever did for yourself.'

'It seems so to you, no doubt; and yet I wish to Heaven that I had never accepted your invitation to come to Halswater.'

'Do you? You prefer potted beef to the flesh-pots of Egypt, and a tent-bed to a spring mattress, eh? It's a queer taste. Well, I am sorry I can't offer you a squaw and a wigwam, but you see it can't be done.'

'You were giving me some advice about keeping guard upon my tongue just now,

Edward,' answered the other hoarsely, ' I would remind you to keep yours in check.'

' Tut, tut, you flame up as quickly as a prairie fire. Dick. It would be a bad thing for both of us—but much worse for you—if we were to quarrel. I was wrong to poke fun at you, of course; but once the thing was manifestly over and gone — done with — I thought you would not be so thin-skinned. It is absolutely necessary, however, my dear fellow, that you should understand it *is* done with. It will not do for you to remain here in the same house with this young couple and let them perceive that you have a hankering to cut the bridegroom's throat. It is necessary that the course of true love should, in this case, not only run smooth, but quickly and without distraction. If you have any doubt of your own self-command I will send you to some warm place—not to the devil, as some people would, but to the Isle of Wight or Torquay, for the recovery of your health, for a month or two; then, when they are married and settled, you could come back again.'

'No, no,' pleaded the other passionately; 'let me be with her as long as I can; it won't be long in any case. I give you my word of honour that neither of them shall ever guess——'

'Take a drop of brandy, Dick,' said his brother, pouring him out a wineglassful, and looking at him as he sat speechless and breathless, with genuine interest. The recollection had come into his mind of a somewhat similar scene with his old partner 'Josh,' to whom he had administered the same remedy! The parallel, however, was not complete; there was nothing the matter in the case of his present patient with the heart itself, but only that its emotion had overpowered him.

'Don't let us talk about this matter any more, my good fellow,' he continued soothingly; 'your word is passed and I can rely on you.'

Grace's first act on finding herself alone that night was to finish her letter to Mrs. Lindon ; its conclusion, it need scarcely be said, was different from that she had proposed to herself a few hours ago, and declined that lady's invitation to visit her. There would be a guest at home (though she did not give that as her excuse), whom she would not have left for many Mrs. Lindons.

Rip was always accustomed to sleep in his young mistress's boudoir, but on this occasion he changed his quarters ; she took his wool-lined basket into her own room, and as he lay there hunting for sweetmarts in his dreams— and with a much better chance of catching one than when awake—she sat far into the night regarding him with tender eyes, and thinking of him who had once saved her life at hazard of his own. But not of him alone. More than once the tenderness was dissolved in tears, and then it was not with Walter Sinclair that her thoughts were occupied, but with that other, who had also been her lover, and on whom cruel death had laid its sudden hand in his youth and strength. Never more would his blithe voice gladden human ear, nor his comeliness delight the eyes of all who beheld it! It is only a very few of us whose life affects ' the gaiety of nations,' but it might be truly said of Lord Cheribert that into whatever company he came he had brought gaiety with him. Moreover, to Grace at least he had disclosed a heart tender and true, and capable of noble deeds (though, alas! they had never been accomplished), and of generous thoughts, which, let us hope, did not perish with him. What had become of them, she wondered, her mind straying into unaccustomed fields of thoughts; and of *him*?

CHAPTER XXXIV

A WELCOME

EVEN the next morning, when those dark thoughts of Death would probably have been swept away by the Light that was to bring love with it—for she knew that Walter was to be asked to the Hall that day—they were fated to still remain with her; for before his arrival she received a letter from Mr. Allerton, of which Lord Cheribert's death was the keynote.

'I have had no time to write to you of late, dear Grace, nor even the heart to write. I have of course been overwhelmed with business in connection with poor Lord Cheribert's affairs, but his loss itself is what has still more occupied it. If I had not been a witness to

his poor father's misery, I might have written.
I have grieved for the lad as if he had been
my own son. I liked him exceedingly, and
there was another reason, of which I cannot
forbear to speak, why my sympathies were
enlisted in his future: his heart was devoted
to one whom I love even better. I have no
reason to suppose that his attachment was returned—I hope *now* that it was not so—but I
know that he was a great favourite of yours,
and that you esteemed his noble nature, and
perceived those great merits in him of which
few persons, save you and me, were cognisant.
I confess that I had looked forward to a time
when you and he—but, alas, " all these things
have ceased to be," and it is worse than useless
to dwell upon them ; but I know that there is
at least one genuine mourner for him beside
myself and his father. As regards the latter
his fate is an awful lesson to us to be patient
with the erring, " especially with those of our
own household." His wretchedness wrings

my heart. I do not, however, write these lines, dear Grace, to make you sorrowful. I would rather remind you that it is not intended that any loss which Providence inflicts upon us should permanently sadden our lives, and least of all when, as in your case, they are but beginning.'

It was a characteristic letter throughout; a curious blending of kindness and good sense, of Christian teaching and the wisdom of this world. Grace read it with remorse, for, though its expressions of regret came home to her every one, she was conscious of being in an altogether different frame of mind from that in which the writer expected to find her. How could it be otherwise, when she was about to meet the man of her choice, for the first time in that acknowledged relation ? She felt that she would be a hypocrite and a dissembler if she did not write that very day to enlighten the good lawyer as to the real state of the case.

Mr. Roscoe had been commissioned by Agnes to send a letter by hand to Dale End that morning to invite Walter to exchange his quarters at the Angler's Rest for a lodging in the cottage, and that young gentleman did not take long in settling his very moderate bill and packing his portmanteau. There was a phrase in the letter, which, though not remarkable for grace of expression, made him think more highly of the writer than he had hitherto done, though, as we know, he had always seemed more sensible of his merits than they deserved.

'We shall all be glad to see you again,' he wrote, 'and one of us (I think between ourselves) particularly so.' It was a little precipitating matters, perhaps, but Mr. Roscoe was personally interested in the dénouement of this idyll, and, as he expressed it to himself, was not going to let there be any shilly-shallying about it, so far as he was concerned.

It so happened that Grace took her walk

by the lakeside that morning, and, meeting the dogcart with Mr. Atkinson and Walter in it, the former was directed to drive on to the Hall (which he did with his tongue in his cheek, and a world of cunning enjoyment in his eyes), and the latter got out and accompanied Grace home on foot: an equivalent in the way of public notice, as far as mine host of the Angler's Rest was concerned, to the publication of their banns in the parish church. The young couple, however, never wasted a thought on this—though public notice was just then the last thing they desired—but pursued their way with happy hearts and the most perfect mutual understanding.

'Agnes and Philippa have been both so kind,' murmured the young lady, *à propos des bottes*, as it would have seemed to most ears.

'And I must say Roscoe has expressed himself in a very friendly way, my darling,' returned Walter in the same dove-like tones, and without the slightest difficulty in detecting her meaning.

What a walk that was by the crisp and sparkling lake in the late autumn morning! For them it had no touch of winter, and in the dark and wintry days that fell upon them —but of whose advent they had no suspicion, for we are speaking not of the changes of the seasons but of the cold and gloom that was fated to embitter their near future—it recurred to their memories again and again with sad distinctness. There was no need for the one to woo or the other to be wooed ; their hearts were wedded already. They were in paradise, and dreamt not of the flaming sword that was to drive them out of it. Their talk would not perhaps have been very interesting to the outsider ; but to themselves every syllable was sweet as the honey of Hybla. When we are reading our own verses aloud, says a great poetess, ' the chariot wheels jar in the gates through which we drive them forth,' and something of the sort takes place in love language, but the speakers are unconscious of it, nay, its very imperfections, the breaks and stops, the half-finished sentences (closed perhaps by a kiss), the wild and wandering vows that Love in its intoxication dictates, seem eloquence itself to them.

As they now moved slowly homewards (not arm-in-arm, for somehow Walter's arm had strayed round Grace's waist), another couple watched them from an elevation of the road that intervened between them and the Hall. They were not outwardly so demonstrative in their attachment to one another, but to judge by their conversation were nevertheless on very familiar terms.

'There come the two turtle doves,' observed Mr. Roscoe (for it was he and Philippa); 'I am glad to see that they are billing and cooing already. If " happy's the wooing that's not long a doing," they will have something to be congratulated upon.'

'I hope so, indeed,' sighed Philippa. 'Though even then I don't see the end of our own trouble.'

'It will be a very satisfactory event in itself at all events,' observed her companion.

'You mean in a pecuniary point of view, I suppose,' returned Philippa gloomily. 'I sometimes wish that there was no such thing as money.'

'If you add "or the want of it," I will agree with you,' responded her companion dryly. 'But their marriage will do much for us, I hope. It will certainly be one of two obstacles removed from our path.'

'But how far the lesser one,' remarked Philippa, with such a deep-drawn sigh that it seemed almost like a groan of despair.

'That is true enough,' he answered, with knitted brow, 'but it is not you, remember, who suffer from Agnes, as I do. *You* are not pestered with her importunities and her impatience. She does not overwhelm *you* with her unwelcome attentions ; indeed,' he added with his grimmest smile, ' you seem of late to be more free from anything of the sort than ever.'

'It may be a laughing matter to you, but not to me, Edward,' she answered angrily. ' You don't know what a woman feels who is situated as I am ; and it seems to me that you don't much care.'

' Nay, nay, do not say that, my dear,' he replied in his most honeyed tone. ' I feel for you very much.'

' To see her coming between me and you,' continued Philippa vehemently, and without taking notice of this blandishment, ' as though she had a right to do it, drives me half frantic ; to have to set a guard all day upon lip and eye, lest word or glance should betray me to her, is not only irksome to me to the last degree, but humiliating. I give you fair warning that I can't stand it much longer.'

She was looking straight before her, and

did not see the scowl that darkened her companion's face; for an instant he wore the look of a demon; it vanished, however, as quickly as it came, and when he spoke it was in the same calm persuasive voice—though with perhaps a little more firmness in it—that had served his turn so often.

. 'My dear Philippa, you seem to have forgotten that this annoyance, of which you not unnaturally complain, was foreseen by us from the first. You made up your mind, you said, to bear it. Under other circumstances we might even have had to bear it longer; I need hardly remind you how *that* necessity was put an end to.'

'Great Heaven, how can you speak of it?' cried Philippa, with a low piteous cry. Her face had grown ghastly white to the very lips, and her eyes expressed an unspeakable horror. 'You promised me you never, never would!'

'Pardon me, my dear, I had forgotten,' he

murmured penitently; 'I should not have done it.'

But the while she hid her face in her hands and sobbed hysterically, the expression on his own was by no means one of penitence. It was, on the contrary, one of satisfaction, and could it have been translated into words would have run, 'Now I have given her something to think about, which will prevent her dwelling upon these little inconveniences for some time to come.' And indeed it seemed he had, for not a word more did she say concerning them, while the young couple drew nearer and nearer.

'Dry your eyes,' whispered Mr. Roscoe sharply and suddenly, 'Agnes is following us.'

This precaution Philippa had hitherto neglected to take. Perhaps she had concluded that there was no necessity for it, since Grace might naturally enough have ascribed her emotion (for Philippa, unlike her elder sister, was very emotional) to pleasure at seeing her with her lover; but she took it now, and, after pressing her handkerchief to her eyes, fluttered it in the wind, as though she had only taken it out in sign of pleasure to the happy pair.

Then she greeted Walter effusively. 'So glad to see you again amongst us, Mr. Sinclair,' and kissed Grace.

Then Agnes joined them with a smile on her face, but not without an expression on it also that betrayed the recent presence of a frown.

'I had hoped to be the first to bid you welcome to Halswater,' she said, 'but I perceive that I have been anticipated.'

By whom was made clear enough by the angry glance she cast at Philippa.

Before that lady could make what would have probably been no very conciliatory rejoinder, Mr. Roscoe struck in.

'We happened to be walking this way,' he observed apologetically.

That use of the plural pronoun, associating, as it did, himself with Philippa, overcame the slight self-restraint that Agnes was putting upon herself. 'I was not referring to you, Mr. Roscoe,' she replied; 'you are not the master of the Hall, and therefore not in a position to welcome any of its guests.'

'You are extremely rude and very offensive, Agnes,' exclaimed Philippa furiously.

'Hush, hush,' said Mr. Roscoe reprovingly; 'you are wrong, Miss Philippa, to speak so to your sister, and Miss Agnes is perfectly right. I must have seemed to her, no doubt—though she was mistaken in so thinking—to have taken too much upon myself,' and he removed his hat and bowed to Agnes.

Her face was a spectacle; it was evident that she bitterly regretted having lost her temper, but that the presence of Philippa prevented her from acknowledging it. To have thus humiliated Mr. Roscoe was pain and grief to her, but she could not humiliate herself by saying so; she looked as though she could have bitten her tongue out. It was an unpleasant quarter of a minute for everybody.

Even Walter Sinclair felt that there were crumpled rose leaves—not to say serpents—in the paradise he had pictured himself as being about to enter.

'It is beautiful weather for the end of October,' he observed, with ludicrous inappositeness; but as any stick does to beat a dog with, so any remark in circumstances of painful embarrassment is seized upon and made use of as a way out of it.

The whole party began talking of autumn tints as though they were peripatetic landscape painters, and had come down to illustrate the neighbourhood.

But in one heart there was such a passion at work—wild rage and cruel hate, and wounded pride, and passionate desire to be even with the cause of his humiliation—that if it could have been laid bare to the eyes of her companions would have frozen the well-meant platitudes upon their lips with the horror of it.

'Philippa is right,' muttered Edward Roscoe to himself, with a frightful oath ; ' this state of things shall not go on much longer.'

END OF THE SECOND VOLUME.

PRINTED BY
SPOTTISWOODE AND CO., NEW-STREET SQUARE
LONDON

www.ingramcontent.com/pod-product-compliance
Lightning Source LLC
Chambersburg PA
CBHW031045120726
47905CB00007B/2315